Pink &
Patent Leather

When the Fall from the Pedestal Isn't Far Enough

A Novel

Candy Jackson

BROWN GIRLS PUBLISHING

Pink & Patent Leather © 2014 by Candy Jackson
Brown Girls Publishing, LLC
www.browngirlspublishing.com

First Brown Girls Publishing LLC trade printing

ISBN-10: 0-9915322-1-X
ISBN-13: 978-0-9915322-1-6

Cover and Interior designed by Jessica Tilles/TWA Solutions.com

Manufactured and Printed in the United States of America

It had been a long time, four years to be exact, but I was ready. The night I had been dreaming about was finally here. My life was playing out like a well-rehearsed script, and I had the starring role.

I wanted a life with him.

It was my time; sweet victory was in the air.

I was Sasha Simone Jansen and I had come to win.

Now, as I sat at my vanity poised and proper with my hair done and make-up flawless, I stared at my perfect cocoa complexion and smiled. I had to be the luckiest girl in the world. No, that wasn't it. I'm a Christian, and we don't believe in luck.

"I'm the most blessed girl in the world," I told my reflection.

From where I sat at my vanity, which was against the far left wall of my blush-colored bedroom, I could see my Christian Dior mini dress on its pink satin-covered hanger. Sitting directly underneath the dress were my black patent leather four-inch stilettos that had a pink bow adorning the right side of both shoes.

I was happy.

Finally.

I had come a long way from being that little flat-chested, a little bit spoiled brat, lovingly known to my family and friends as "Pink." Pink was the nickname given to me by my oldest brother. After having given birth to three sons, God finally blessed my mother with me—her daughter, and pride and joy. I was my daddy's heart, and the apple of my brothers' eyes.

My brother started calling me Pink just a few weeks after I was born. He said that Mother dressed me every day in pink just to make sure that everyone knew that I was a girl.

Now, I was a grown girl, with my Bachelor of Arts degree from Spelman, and my high-rise condominium located in the great metropolis, formerly known as Chocolate City. With my fancy little 525 BMW with custom wheels and personalized tags, I truly was a long way from where I used to be.

Many might think that I am still spoiled, but heck, I had worked hard in college. I remained a permanent fixture on the Dean's list each semester, spent every summer abroad, and graduated magna cum laude with a degree in journalism.

Now, I was a young, rising junior editor at Power Play Magazine, where even though I'd only been there three months, I was on the move. I was flirting, teasing, and proving to my boss that I had beauty, but it was my brains that was going to get me to the top without sleeping with him or any man.

But all of that was my professional life. Now that I had that in order, it was time for me to move to the personal side of the ledger.

Glancing at the brass clock on my nightstand, I saw that I had plenty of time to spare. All of my preparations were in place and I would arrive at the celebration tonight fashionably late.

As if I had an audience watching me, I sauntered over to my bed in nothing but my bashful colored Le Pearle lace thong and matching demi-bra. When I laid down, I let my thoughts wander to him.

I pictured his reaction when we'd finally come face to face once again tonight. It had been so long since he'd seen me. He was going to be surprised, mesmerized, and hopefully hypnotized with what he saw.

Because now, I was a woman.

For four years, I'd stayed away from not only Grace Tabernacle, but I hadn't even come close to the city lines of my hometown of Washington, DC. I never saw my friends, and only saw my parents when they came to Atlanta, which was often since my mother was also a Spelman graduate and my father was a third-generation Morehouse man. My parents loved visiting what they called the new Chocolate City and staying at the Ritz Carlton in Buckhead. That gave them easy access to one of their favorite shopping spots, Phipps Plaza right across the street.

But though I did get to see my parents often, I only saw my brothers at Christmas, which we spent either in Raleigh, Boston, or New York City, which is where each of my brothers lived. Besides my family, though, I saw no one else. I had stayed away from D.C. all because of him. Everything I'd sacrificed, I'd done with him in mind.

I wasn't sad about it, though. He had kept me focused. The entire time I was in college I had just one plan—to get good grades and to get in great shape. So when my roommates tried to get me to go club hopping or to take trips to neighboring colleges for some good old-fashioned fun, I always turned them down.

Instead, I spent my time grooming my mind, body and soul. I studied constantly and when I wasn't studying, I worked out. I plumped up my ass by doing one hundred squats a day, and then I jogged two miles around campus— twice a day. Doing that just about every day for four years had turned me from a girl into a lean, mean, toned woman.

Then, with the money my parents sent as a weekly allowance, I took to the neighboring town and patronized the best hair salon, purchasing top-of-the-line conditioners and relaxers that had added nearly fourteen inches to my cinnamon-colored tresses.

From there, I'd spend hours at the day spa getting silk-wrapped manicures, coconut-oil pedicures, and full body hot rock muscle massages that became second nature to me. I had regular herbal facials, and of course, there was the honey waxing of my arms, legs, and yes, even my kitty.

It had all paid off.

I looked incredible and it was all for Pastor Malik Stroman, the most handsome, smartest, put-together man that I'd ever met.

He'd changed my life, all those years ago. It was a revelation that had come to me in a single moment, six years before.

I was only sixteen then, when the "Mothers" of the church were preparing nine of us girls in the ladies lounge for our special ceremony. The women made sure our dresses were pressed, that our shoes glistened, and that every strand of our hair was in place. While the women prepared the other girls, I stood off to the side. I wouldn't dare let one of them touch me. There was no need, my mother had already made sure that I was perfect.

But, I also stood away from the others because I didn't fit in. I had never fit in with the girls I went to school with or sat with in Sunday school. Not that I wanted to. I couldn't relate to their J. C. Penney dresses, Rack Room shoes, and chit-chatter about the teenage boys in our church. I had nothing in common with any of them.

That wasn't my fault. My parents were the ones who'd set me apart from the very beginning. I'd been wearing designer clothes since I could read labels. I'd had weekly visits to the hair salon since I was five, and just a few weeks before for my sixteenth birthday, my mother and father had given me my first brand-new car.

So, there was just no way for me to relate to those girls or for those girls to relate to me.

"Okay, come on now." Ms. Pearl clapped her hands three times as she motioned for us to gather together in a small circle. "Let's pray."

Even though they had placed small pillows on the floor so that we could kneel without messing up our stockings or our dresses, I sat on the settee in the corner of the lounge. My mother had spent three hundred dollars on my dress and not even praying was going to get me anywhere close to the floor.

Each of the Mothers prayed over us and then, they lined us up and led us into the darkened sanctuary that was brightened only by hundreds of flickering candles. As we passed through the doors, two of the Deacons stood at the entryway and gave each of us a white rose. But when I'd only taken two steps, my white rose was quickly replaced by a pink one, courtesy of my oldest brother who'd flown in from North Carolina for the occasion.

We marched slowly down the aisle, and even with the dim candle light, I could see that every seat in the church was taken.

The nine of us moved to the altar and when I got to the front, Pastor Malik, who was dressed in a long burgundy robe looked down at me and smiled. I smiled back noticing that he hadn't seemed to take interest in any of the other girls.

When we all stood in place, our fathers joined us, each man standing behind his daughter.

"Let us join together, and give praise unto The Lord," Pastor Malik said as he raised his hands in the air.

Then, the choir director played the opening chords and together, the congregation sang, "Lord, prepare me to be a sanctuary, pure and holy, tried and true..."

I closed my eyes and swayed as I sang unto God, asking him to prepare me, to lead me not into temptation, and to purify me. This was a song, but it felt like a prayer, and I was so serious about the words and the vow that I was about to take.

When the Minister of Music hit the last chords on the keyboard, praises went up behind me as people shouted,

"Hallelujah," "Praise you, Lord," and, "Amen!"

It took a couple of minutes for the sanctuary to be quiet once again, and then, Pastor Malik began.

"Saints, please bow your heads."

I lowered my head until my chin hit my chest.

"Father, for these are your daughters, your children, and they present themselves to you on this day, making the sacrifice of abstinence."

My eyes were closed, but then, I opened one eye, just a little, and peeked at the pastor. And for some reason, my heart began to beat just a little bit faster. I watched him as his words poured out.

From the time Pastor Malik had come to this church two years before, I'd admired him. First, he was young, at least he was young compared to all the old ministers who'd been at Grace Tabernacle before. Pastor Malik was in his twenties, and I'd never met a preacher so young before. His age alone made him cool.

Then, I found out all of his social vital statistics: he was Harvard-educated, his father was a well-known Bishop in our church district. His mother had been a social advocate, with her primary focus raising awareness and money for a cure for breast cancer.

Of course, all of that impressed me. Until I heard him preach. I had never heard anyone preach like him before. First of all, he kind of sang the message instead of talking. And then, I loved everything that he preached. He talked about God as part of our lives today. He talked about God as if God were living and breathing right now. After listening to Pastor

Malik, every week, I felt closer to The Lord. To me, he was a smart and wonderful man of God.

"These young women, Lord, are promising that they will wait on you, God, to send them a mate before they engage in holy lovemaking."

When he said, 'lovemaking,' my knees got weak. But I was able to hold myself up as Pastor Malik ended his prayer and then stepped in front of the first girl in line. He said a few words to each girl as he took the ring from her father, slipped it onto her finger, then gave her a soft kiss on her cheek.

With each step that Pastor Malik took toward me, my breathing quickened and I began to tremble. By the time he stood in front of me, I could hardly stand.

"Sweet Pink," Pastor Malik said he looked into my eyes.

I felt like I was being hypnotized.

He took my ring from my father. "You're growing up to be such a fine young lady. It is wonderful that you're doing this and I want you to know that God is pleased." Then, he lifted my hand and instead of placing the ring on my finger, he brought the back of my hand to his lips and gave me a kiss.

I almost fainted as I smelled his minty-breath against my flesh. But, I kept my eyes on his as he spoke.

"True love waits," he said, as he gently slipped the platinum band with diamond chips onto my finger. "I am proud that you have decided to save yourself for marriage."

That was when it happened, right then, at that moment, in that instant. It was like I was being washed in this overwhelming feeling that God had a message for me.

The man of God for you has been chosen!

The voice was so loud, so clear that I wanted to look around to see who had spoken that to me.

And then, the voice came again: *The man of God for you has been chosen.*

In just a few seconds, I had a conversation with God: This man? I asked.

The man of God for you has been chosen.

I guess God felt like He had already made it clear, and all I needed to do was receive the message—Pastor Malik was the man that God had chosen for me!

My heart was filled with such joy and when Pastor Malik leaned forward to kiss my cheek, I had to tell him what God had told me. My pastor needed to know what had been placed on my heart.

So as he was still bent over, I whispered, "I'm saving myself for you, Malik. This is all for you."

The way his head snapped back and his eyes widened, I could tell that I startled him, surprised him, stunned him. But he was quick; he recovered and played it off. Although, he did lose his smile just a little bit when he looked at my father and reached to shake his hand.

I guessed that Pastor Malik was a little worried that my father had heard what I'd said. But, I wasn't concerned at all. First of all, I'd said it softly enough because my words were for his ears only. But even if my daddy had heard me, it wouldn't have mattered. Bishop Dr. Richard Jansen always saw to it that I got everything that I wanted.

What I wanted was Pastor Malik Stroman. As I stood there at the altar, all I wanted was his hands on my body, his lips on my flesh, and I wanted to be inside his masculine embrace for long moments of heated passion.

It didn't matter how old he was or how young I was, or even that he was married. All that mattered was I always had the best of everything, and in my eyes, and the eyes of everyone he came in contact with, Pastor Malik was the best. And the best should have the best—at least, that's what The Lord and I thought.

I had no concerns about his wife because this was all God's plan. And anyway, how he'd married her in the first place was a mystery to me. She wasn't anywhere close to being the best; she didn't deserve him. Honestly, I couldn't figure out how he ended up with that frumpy, old-looking, tacky, nappy-headed, dumb ass woman. He deserved better, he deserved me.

Even as Pastor Malik went back to the center of the altar and gave the closing words to the ceremony, God continued to speak to my heart.

Sasha, prepare yourself to become the First Lady.

And so, from that night on that's exactly what I did. I knew if I heard God tell me, surely God must have told him, too. That's why I'd spent all these years getting ready. Tonight was the manifestation of all the work I'd done. My assignment was complete, almost.

Rolling over on the bed, I glanced once again at the clock on my night table. It was seven-thirty. Perfect.

It was time for me to get dressed and go stake my claim.

Chapter 2

I was wearing this Christian Dior dress. Everything about it (and me in it) was perfect. The black sleeveless sheath showed my perfectly toned "Michelle Obama" arms, and the mid-thigh length revealed shapely legs that looked like they went on forever. My four-inch Jimmy Choos that made me appear super-model tall, only added to the whole affect.

As I stared at my reflection in the mirror, I tried to imagine Pastor Malik's reaction. Would he see that I was ready for him, ready in every way?

That question took a little bit of air from my lungs and I sat on the edge of my bed. There was so much at stake, and I took a moment to think about all that was going to happen tonight, tomorrow, this week, this month, this year. Though, it was going to be tough, and I knew some people would be hurt (especially my parents who were pillars of the church and their community) I had to follow through with what God had put on my heart. I was glad, though, that my parents weren't going to be there tonight. They had just left the day before for a two-week vacation in Fiji. My hope was that by the time they returned, the news would be waiting for them. The deed would already be done.

I did hope that my parents weren't going to be too affected, though I'd be crazy to think that there wouldn't be any trouble. It wasn't like I was taking this journey blindly; I knew that people would be shocked, and some might be hurt. That's why I'd been so careful in planning every step from the moment I'd uttered those words to Pastor Malik at the Purity Ceremony.

For the first few weeks after that night, whenever Pastor Malik saw me in church, he was a bit standoffish, as if he was concerned (or afraid) that I might say (or do) something that would embarrass him. But he never had to worry. God had spoken, and I would never do anything that I wasn't supposed to do. And at that time, all I was supposed to do was prepare myself. I was only sixteen, I had plenty of time, and so I just acted as if I had never spoken those words to him. I behaved as if nothing had changed when everything *had* changed.

After awhile, Pastor Malik relaxed and returned to the relationship we'd had before that night. For the next two years, I was just sweet little Pink to him. He came to my high school graduation party, and even the little gathering my parents had for me the night before I left for Spelman.

"Make sure you stay in touch," Pastor Malik had said as he hugged me goodbye. "Unless of course, you meet one of those Morehouse guys down there and get too busy."

Everyone had laughed at that little joke, except for me. I didn't know why Pastor Malik would say something like that. Of course, that would never happen; I would never get involved with a boy when I already had a man.

But then, I realized that he was just saying that for the benefit of his wife, who was always with him, always hanging on as if she was afraid someone was going to steal him away.

I guess she had a very good reason to be worried. God had probably told her, too. God had probably told her that she was just my place-holder and that I was going to be Malik's wife.

So, I didn't say anything as everyone laughed at Malik's joke. Then the next day, I left for college. When I walked out of the door of my home, I knew that I wouldn't be coming back. Not for four years. I hadn't shared my plans not to return with anyone, but staying away was a necessary part. The next four years had to be transformational years. I had to turn myself into the woman that God wanted me to be for Pastor Malik. I was going to be smart, I was going to be beautiful, I was going to be ready to be the most awesome First Lady in America.

My plan was to stay away physically, but I wasn't going to disconnect myself from Pastor Malik totally. Keeping it casual, I sent him weekly updates through handwritten letters on what I had been doing around campus because after all, he needed to be involved in the life of his future wife. So, I told him about my studies and my desire to be the best student I could possibly be. And then, I told him about the all-girls Wednesday night Bible study that I started in the Student Union building.

With every letter I sent, Pastor Malik would email back to me and I cherished every single message from him:

Wow, Pink. I'm impressed. I want to support you in this endeavor, so I've included some study guides and other material that you can download and use at the Bible study. I'm very proud of you and the work that you're doing for The Lord.

I was ecstatic when I received that. He was already beginning to see the asset I was going to be to him.

Each time, I wrote back (because written letters were much more personal to me), always thanking him for his support and always stamping my notes with my signature perfume, Jadore by Dior and signing, *Yours in Christ, Pink.*

Then, in the first week of my senior year, Pastor Malik sent an email that said:

You're getting closer to graduation, Pink. Although I've missed seeing you, I can't wait to see the young woman that you've become.

I almost cried when I read those words. This let me know that even though Pastor Malik hadn't seen me, he knew the reason why I had stayed away. He understood that I was preparing myself. So, I sent him back a note, and told him that I couldn't wait to see him either. This time, though, after I stamped the note with my perfume, I changed up my signature and signed, *Love, Pink. Always at your service.*

I wondered if Pastor Malik would notice the difference—and he did. I got an email back from him faster than ever before. As I sat in my dorm room, my whole body shook with anticipation when I saw that I had a new email from him. What message had Pastor Malik sent back? Was he ready to talk about us, since I would be home in a nine months?

But when I opened his email, I had to read it a couple of times to make sure that I hadn't missed something:

Pink, there's a young man I want you to meet. He's a graduate of Howard, and he joined Grace Tabernacle the first year you were away. There's a call on his life to become a minister and right now, he's down at Morehouse completing his final year of law school. His name is Xavier Turner and he's looking forward to hearing from you.

There was an email and a telephone number at the bottom of the note.

What the heck was this? That was my first thought. Was he trying to set me up with another man? Was he trying to push me away?

I read that message over and over, trying to read between the lines, trying to see the message that I'd clearly missed. But even after studying it for two days, I could only come to one conclusion—Pastor Malik was acting like he didn't want us to be together.

But why? Why wasn't he following the plan that God had for our lives?

Then, I began to wonder, what if this was a test? What if Pastor Malik just wanted to see if I would be obedient? As his wife, I'd have to be submissive and maybe he was trying to see if I understood that.

So three days after receiving his note, I called Xavier Turner.

"I've been waiting to hear from you, Sasha," he said, surprising me by calling me by my given name.

"You can call me Pink," I said. "All of my friends do."

"Great!"

We made plans that night to meet at Starbucks the next day and I arrived early because if he looked like a reject from an old sitcom, I was going to sneak out, run, and then change my number.

But when Xavier walked through the door, I stayed right in my seat. He was way too fine, way too cut-up, and had way too much swagger to be anybody's minister. Old boy was hell-a-gorgeous with a broad chest, arms that gave new meaning to the word, "guns," a small waist and long, sturdy legs. He was at least, six-feet-four with a creamy caramel complexion, that set off his yellow Ralph Lauren polo shirt that went well with his navy slacks. Oh my goodness, he was everything!

"Pink?" he asked after he stepped right over to me.

I nodded, not at all surprised that he'd picked me out. It was true that Atlanta had some beautiful women, but I stood out. I wasn't bragging, that was just a fact. I had worked hard to be a cut above the rest.

Xavier hadn't been sitting across from me for five minutes before I felt like I'd known him forever. Talking to him was easy. We shared the same interests, like politics, old school music, and reading all of the classics. He was well-read, well-traveled and knew African American history almost as well as I did. But what really sealed the deal for me was when he challenged me to a game of chess. My brothers had taught me how to play when I was just five, and I could take on...and win, the very best chess players.

What seemed to impress him most about me was my knowledge of the Bible and the sessions I was doing with my fellow students.

"So, not only are you well-read," he said, "but you read your Bible, too. That's what I'm talking about."

"I love The Lord." That was all I said and it wasn't just a cliché. I really did love God. Not only had I been raised in the church, but I knew and studied God for myself. From the time I was a little girl, He'd laid things on my heart, and what He was doing with me and Malik was just proof that His love for me continued.

Xavier said, "I love the Bible study that you're doing. I would love to do something like that for guys."

"Maybe we can do something together," I said, sipping my Chai Latte.

Before we left that Starbucks that day, Xavier and I had come up with a plan to do an early morning prayer line with the girls at Spelman and the guys at Morehouse.

Xavier wasn't playing. We started the next morning. I was barely awake when he called me at six am, and then, we started adding people to the line. Three weeks later, we had to get a conference number where everyone could just call in, that's how many people were on the line with us.

That's how our wonderful friendship started, with prayer.

I'd grown up, feeling so separated from the girls my age. I'd never had anyone that I'd called a friend, let alone a best friend.

But Xavier had quickly become that kind of friend to me. I could talk to him, I could relate to him. We spent all of our time together, studying, eating, and we even worked out together. And when we weren't together, we were on the phone talking to each other.

So I was shocked when right before the Christmas holidays, Xavier and I were at the CNN Center, just walking around, people watching, taking in the holiday scene, and he said to me, "We should go out."

I laughed. "What are you talking about? We're already out."

"No, I mean. We should go out...together. Just you and me."

It still took me a couple of moments for me to get what he was saying. I was slow to answer because I wanted to come correct. And especially since he was my best friend, I wanted to tell him the truth.

"I can't do that, Xavier."

The way his eyebrows rose, I could tell he was surprised by my answer. "Why not? Are you seeing someone that I don't know about?" He laughed and I knew why he did. It would've been impossible for me to be seeing someone else with the amount of time that I spent with him.

"No, it's not that, but you're close." When he frowned, I added, "It's not that I'm seeing someone else because I don't have to. God has already shown me the man who's going to be my husband."

A couple of seconds went by before Xavier said, "Wow." Then, after a pause, he said, "Well, first of all, I didn't ask you to marry me."

"I know that, but it doesn't make sense to start something that we can't finish."

"Okay, I get that, but where's this man that God has shown you? Why don't you spend time with him?"

"It's complicated," I said, knowing that there was no way I could say anymore. When it was time for Pastor Malik and I to come out to the world, we would do that together. "You have to trust me, and believe me," I added. "I love you as a friend, but it can never be anything more."

Xavier had said, "All right," that night. But he never gave up.

The thing was, though, even if God hadn't chosen my husband for me already, it could never be X. He didn't have the same up-bringing and for me, that would never do. He was nothing more than a common man with a stereotypical tag. Yes, he was an aspiring minister, yes, he was in his last year of law school and was studying to pass the bar, yes, one day he'd be an amazing attorney. But even with all of that, he was no Pastor Malik.

My parents knew that, too. From the day my father first laid his eyes on Xavier my dad felt "that boy" was no good. My mother and father had actually met Xavier before I did.

"Pastor stood at the altar," my father began to tell me the story, "and gave the invitation for anyone who wanted to join the church to come forward. That boy strutted down the aisle like he was at some rap concert rather than in the Lord's Holy place. Every woman in that sanctuary from five to ninety-five sat up and paid attention." My father had shaken his head like the whole thing still disgusted him. "But he didn't fool me, baby girl. I know his kind and his kind is not good enough for you."

That was my father's warning to me when I'd told him and my mother about the young minister I'd been introduced to by Pastor Malik. Once my father realized that I was talking about Xavier, he wanted to make sure that I wasn't interested in anything besides having a cup of coffee with Xavier.

My father continued his case against Xavier like he was in court, "I can't even believe that my alma mater accepted him. Morehouse must be lowering their standards."

My dad didn't have anything to worry about. Even though he was about to be a lawyer and pastor, I was never going to get with Xavier, though I did hope that we would always be friends.

I had to blink a couple of times to bring myself back to the present, back to my bedroom. But even though my mind was back on what I was going to do tonight with Pastor Malik, Xavier was still on my mind. My parents were going to be very hurt by what I was going to do, but Xavier would be the one who was hurt most of all.

But that wasn't completely my fault. Even though I'd tried to warn X, there were times when we did behave like boyfriend and girlfriend. Especially when our friendship had turned kind of intimate. We'd gone from kissing, to fondling, to other things that most girls only did with their boyfriends. But I'd never done those things for my physical pleasure nor for Xavier's. Everything I did in my life had one purpose only—Pastor Malik. And the only reason I'd gone that far with Xavier was that it made sense to me to be ready for Pastor Malik in every way. Because once we were together, I had to be sure that I was better in bed with him than his wife had been.

So with Xavier, I practiced a lot. Of course, while there were things that I did with my mouth, I was still a virgin. Only Pastor Malik would have me in that way.

When I glanced at my bedside clock, I couldn't believe that only fifteen minutes had passed since I'd gotten dressed. So many thoughts had gone through my mind, I felt like I'd relived the last nine months with Xavier.

Now though, it was time for my new beginning. It was time to put the past behind me and step into my future. It was time for Pastor Malik Stroman to see the woman that Sasha Simone Jansen had become.

I slid the chain-strap of my designer bag onto my shoulder, grabbed the gift that I'd bought, then clasped my fingers over the handle of my overnight bag. I was finally ready to go.

Chapter 3

Pulling in front of the Willard Hotel didn't stop my nerves. Even though Pastor Malik was my mission, Xavier was still on my mind. How would he react to all of this? Would he figure it out right away? Would he be hurt or would he be angry?

I truly hoped that Xavier *wouldn't* be hurt, but if he were, all he had to do was look back and remember all that I'd told him. He'd see that I'd always been honest and upfront. X was the one who had settled for whatever bone I'd tossed his way.

Although I was anxious, I was really looking forward to the freedom that tonight would bring. The smoke would clear, and for the first time everyone, including Xavier would have clarity. Everyone would see what I'd seen all along. Everyone would see God's plan in action.

As I waited for the valet attendant to come over to my car, I rested my head against the headrest embossed with a capital "P." I was already feeling exhausted and this night hadn't even started yet. What had me most nervous was that I didn't have any idea how this night was going to end.

When the attendant came over to my car and opened the door, I reached over the passenger seat and picked up the gift that I had for Pastor Malik. Then, I slid my legs out and noticed the way the young guy's eyes dropped. His eyes moved from my legs, all the way up when I stepped completely out of my BMW.

"Welcome...to the...Willard," he stuttered.

"Thank you. I'm here for Pastor Malik Stroman's Anniversary Celebration."

"Yes. That's in the Crystal ballroom."

"Thank you," I said as I tucked my ticket into my purse. "I need you to do me a favor and keep my car right here in the front. I won't be long," I told the man.

I waited until he nodded before I turned away. Having my car right here was an important part of my plan. There were two ways that this could go and one of the outcomes would cause me to make a quick getaway.

As I sauntered into the hotel, I felt the valet attendant's eyes on me. Once I stepped into the lobby, I felt even more people turning to take a look as I strolled through the hotel. I was used to the attention, but none of it ever mattered to me. I lived for only one man's reaction.

The Willard had always been one of my daddy's favorite places to dine, and tonight, as I made my way to the ballroom I did what I had done so many times as a child. I marveled at the striking green columns and the dazzling crystal chandeliers that hung perfectly over my head. The turn of the century opulence of the hotel helped me to understand clearly that my parents had raised me in the fashion of royalty.

Stepping off of the elevator, I took one final, long cleansing breath before I entered the ballroom. The space was packed with at least five hundred members of Grace Tabernacle, though I wasn't surprised. This was a celebration to honor Pastor Malik for his ten years in the ministry. He had come to Grace Tabernacle a young man in his twenties and now he'd matured spiritually and physically into his thirties.

Chatter and light music filled the bright room as I made my way through the crowd. I'd been going to Grace Tabernacle since I was a child, so there were many familiar faces. But I was careful not to make eye contact with anyone. And no one stopped me because they weren't quite sure if this was me. I hadn't been home in four years, and though my face had stayed the same, the rest of me was a complete transformation.

I pushed my way through the maze of tables as people stood around talking. It looked like dinner had already been served. That meant that the program was about to begin.

Like everything else in my life, this was perfect. Perfect timing.

My view to the front of the ballroom was blocked with all of the people milling around. But then after just a couple of turns, I saw him. Pastor Malik sat at the dais, gracing everyone with a smile that was bright and filled with love.

That made me smile, too, although for a second, my joy faded when I saw his wife, sitting next to him. Of course, she would be there; she was always there. But I was happy again when I turned my attention back to him.

Malik was more handsome than I remembered, more regal because now he sported a very low trimmed beard. His brown complexion glowed and his smile was "rock star" perfect. The tux he wore finished his look of pure sophistication.

It made me want him all the more.

"Pink, is that you?"

I turned around to face Mother Pearl, who looked exactly the same as she did six years ago, on the day she prepared me and the rest of the girls for the Purity Ceremony. She looked about ninety-years-old then, and she looked about ninety-nine-years-old now.

"That is you," she exclaimed. Even though I towered over her, she pulled me to her ample breasts. She squeezed me so tight, I wondered if she was purposely trying to smother me.

"It's good to see you," I said, even though right now, that wasn't true. I didn't want to see anyone except for Pastor Malik.

"It's good to see you, chile. We're so glad to have you home. And so proud of you."

Once Mother Pearl called me out, there were others who took notice, and took my attention away from where I wanted it to be.

But then, when Ms. Odom, the church secretary stood at the mic and announced, "Would all the heads of the ministry please come forward," that was my cue.

"Excuse me," I said to Mother Pearl and the others who stood around me.

This was the part of the program where each of the ministries presented the pastor with a gift. And my gift was going to be as important as anyone's.

My strut was filled with purpose. As I moved toward Pastor Malik, I pretended that I was on the runway during fashion week, and he was the top-of-the-line designer looking for his next million-dollar girl.

He hadn't seen me yet, but his wife did. I could tell from her frown and then the way her eyes widened that it took a moment for complete recognition to set in. Slowly, she rose as if somehow, that was supposed to intimidate me. Her eyes scanned my body, but I kept moving like I didn't care (which I didn't) and that seemed to intimidate her. For just a moment, she looked away from me, and glanced down at herself. What a bad move. She had just put her insecurities on full display and with good reason.

Mrs. Stroman was probably one of the tackiest women at our church. I often wondered about her age because if she was in her thirties like Pastor Malik, I couldn't tell. Especially not from the 1980's-style clothes that she wore.

I'd never seen her hair in any other style than what she was wearing tonight—the greasy curl. It was as if her hair had been set on rollers, then, the curlers were taken out. After that, her hair had been greased, but someone forgot the final step—of styling her hair.

It wasn't just her hairstyle that was a hot mess. That floral printed shift that she wore almost made me laugh out loud. Who wore floral to an evening event? And to top things off, she had on kitten heels. She was so below-average, it hurt my eyes to look at her.

I was still a few feet away from the dais, when she looked away from me and said to her husband, "Here, sweetheart, open this one first."

She handed Pastor Malik the package as if that would keep his attention away from me. Please! He would have to be blind to miss what I was offering.

When I was just a few steps from front and center, I felt a hand on my bare arm. I knew who it was before I even turned and faced him. Xavier. In the moment when our eyes met, I saw his questions, then his understanding, then his indignation.

"I thought you said you weren't feeling well," Xavier whispered. "I thought that's why you said you weren't coming. Why you didn't want to come here with me."

That was the story that I had given him, but Xavier was smart. I could tell by the way he peered through me that his thoughts were going through all kinds of machinations and calculations. And in only a few seconds, he had the answer to the equation that had been in his mind. He said, "Him? Pink, really? Him?"

I didn't part my lips.

"He's the man that you think God...."

He didn't finish his sentence and I still said nothing.

At first, I thought he was going to laugh at me, but his face stayed stern. "You're making a mistake."

As gently as I could, I snatched my arm away and without a word to Xavier, I kept on moving. In just a couple of steps, I was there. Right in front of Pastor Malik.

It was as if my presence stopped everything. No one spoke, no one moved. Everyone just kept their eyes on me.

"Hello Malik." For the first time ever, I left the 'Pastor' from in front of his name. Because it was time.

His eyes squinted just slightly, as if he was trying to hide the way his glance roamed over all of my new womanly curves.

With my eyes on him, I offered my gift to him.

"Thank you, Pink," he said softly. Then, he stood, leaned over and kissed my cheek.

That two second touch sent a spark straight through my body. A spark that settled in the center of my womanhood. A spark that I wasn't expecting.

He sat back down, but his beautiful brown eyes that were dark and soulful and covered with curly, dark lashes, never left me. He watched me, standing there poised and perfect. Even when his wife said, "Sweetheart, you have other gifts you have to open first," he stayed still with his eyes on me.

He ignored his wife's words and lifted the top of the oblong box that I'd given him. His fingers caressed the silk Brooks Brother's tie and then, when he raised the pink tie to his chest, the small platinum ring that I had finally taken off this morning fell into his lap.

At first, his handsome face was carved with lines of confusion. But then, he raised his eyebrows and I knew that he remembered. And he understood.

I stood frozen, excited, and scared. He had to say something, and in a moment, I would know whether those words I'd spoken six years ago had haunted him or inspired him.

He said, "Thank you, Sister Pink."

It wasn't his words that got to me. It was what happened next. It was his smile. His bright, wide smile that was meant just for me.

It was on!

I waited just another moment, just in case he was willing to give up everything and come with me right then. But when he didn't move and stayed behind the dais, I understood. He couldn't just walk away from his wife like this. This was going to take planning and time.

That was fine with me. I believed God's word when He said everything decently and in order. I had waited this long. Another night or two wouldn't matter.

I winked, then pivoted, and sauntered away with a whole lot of promise in my strut.

I was about halfway to the door when it dawned on me that just maybe he could have missed the message. So, I stopped, turned back around, and even though half of the ballroom would be able to hear me, I said, "You're welcome, Malik. Anything for you."

Then, I kept walking, making eye contact with no one. I didn't stop when I got to the ballroom door. I didn't even stop to wait for the elevator, instead, taking the stairs. I didn't stop until I got to the front of the hotel and handed the valet my ticket for my car.

The same attendant who'd helped me out of my car, helped me back in and I gave him a twenty-dollar tip before I glanced in my rearview mirror and then sped away.

It was only then that I breathed. I had expected Xavier to be right behind me, but I made a clean getaway. Wasn't sure if Xavier had followed me, but I was sure that I got away.

When I turned onto Pennsylvania Avenue, I let myself smile. That had gone better than I expected, actually. Even though I hoped, I had never expected tonight to be the actual night. It had been nothing but wishful thinking to believe that Malik could just walk out of his celebration and come with me, although I was absolutely sure that's what he wanted to do. But good things came to those who waited. Malik and I would have our night. Very soon. With the way he had looked at me, I knew that.

Nothing and no one could now stop the inevitable.

It was going to happen.

Chapter 4

Men were so predictable.

Xavier was right in the lobby of the church waiting for me, just the way I knew he would be. Just like I knew that not ten minutes after I got into my car last night, my phone would start blowing up.

And it did. My phone rang and rang. It rang as I pulled up in front of the Four Seasons hotel in Georgetown. It rang while I checked in and even as I followed the bellman who led me to my room. It rang when I settled onto the soft duvet, and it rang when I picked up the remote and clicked on the television. My cell didn't stop ringing until I powered it off. I had never even looked down to check out who was calling me because I knew. Xavier would have called until I answered. And since I had no plans on answering, I had no doubt that he would've just rolled up to my condo, which was exactly why I had checked into a hotel.

Xavier would want to confront me, but I wasn't about to give him a chance, at least not last night. We would have our confrontation, but it was going to be when and where I wanted it.

Part of not wanting to do it last night was because I didn't want to see the immediacy of Xavier's heartbreak. I knew I'd be able to not only see his hurt, but feel it, too. But on the other side, there was a part of me that wanted him to be hurt. I needed him to be hurt. I needed him to think about what had happened all night. I needed him to feel used and cheated. And then, he would be furious, filled with rage, and waiting for me in the lobby of the church—which is exactly where he was.

As I eased my car down the lane that passed right in front of Grace Tabernacle, I could see Xavier through the huge glass doors—pacing, anxiously, prowling the foyer like a lion waiting on his prey. It looked like he was wearing one of the suits, the grey one, that I'd helped him pick out when we'd gone shopping at Lenox Mall right before we came back to DC in May.

His head was down as he paced, as if he was thinking, trying to figure out his next move, and though this was the way I wanted it, I had to admit that I was a bit nervous. It was going to be hard to face him, but this was the plan. Xavier was part of my sacrifice and he had to be one of my casualties.

Taking a final glance at Xavier, I pulled my car into the space that was reserved for my parents. Now, even more than yesterday, I was glad that they were not here to witness all of this. I wanted everything to be complete before they came home and had to face these people.

Even after turning off the ignition, I sat in my car and turned up the volume. As usual, WHUR was doing it, playing the best in Sunday morning music.

"I need you now! I need you now...not another second or another minute..."

I closed my eyes and from my shoulders up, swayed to Smokie Norful's soulful voice. I got into the words, especially the part where he sang about needing God right away. That's how I felt. I needed God now. Because having to face Xavier wasn't going to be easy.

Yes, this was a plan that had come straight from God, but Xavier could be a scary dude. I mean, as handsome as he was, there was no doubt, he had been some places. Sometimes when I looked at him, he reminded me of someone who'd been to prison and who had spent every one of his free hours in the pen working out. I knew that wasn't the case, though.

Xavier had grown up very different from the penitentiary look that he had. Even though he'd been raised by his single mother after his father deserted the family when Xavier was just four years old, his mother was determined to raise Xavier and his brother in a middle class household. She was a secretary in the English department at Morehouse, then after an eight-hour day at the college, she went to work at her part-time job in the Walden's Bookstore in the Greenbriar Mall that was only blocks away from the Southwest Atlanta neighborhood where they lived.

While I always had the love of both my parents who showered me with attention: hugs, kisses, gifts, and the granting of all of my wishes, Xavier's mother didn't have time for all of that with all of the hours that she worked. In fact, X talked more about his grandparents. It was his grandmother and grandfather who took care of them after school, watching over them as they did their homework, making sure they had dinner. And then on Sundays, it was his grandparents who took him to church while his mother rested at home on the only day when she didn't have to work.

Church had made the greatest difference in Xavier's life. "I don't know what it was, Pink," he told me the first day when we'd met, "but in church, that's where I felt complete love, God's love. That's where I found peace. Even as a little boy, that's where I felt the greatest peace of my life."

Well, I hoped that Xavier was feeling a little bit of that peace now as he waited for me. Yeah, I wanted him upset, and I knew he was after listening this morning to the dozens of messages he'd left on my cell—the last one at midnight stating that he was waiting for me at my condo. But, I wanted him to be calm, too. I didn't want him to go off, didn't want him to do anything to hurt me.

"Well, here goes nothing."

As I stepped out of my car, I smiled for the first time this morning. I had parked right next to the space that was soon to be mine. Malik and his wife's spaces were to the left of my parents and I couldn't wait until I'd be pulling my Beamer (or maybe I'd have a Bentley like my parents by then) right next to Malik's Mercedes. This morning, I'd awakened with such a yearning for him, such a strong need to be close to him. I was thinking that there was no need to wait. Maybe I could have Malik in my bed by tonight.

Slowly walking up the steps to the front, I could see my reflection in the glass doors. Today, I was wearing my Sunday best...which was much more conservative than what I'd worn last night. Well, if you could call my hot pink, knee-length, St. John's knit that hugged my hips and dipped in at my sides, conservative. That probably wasn't the right word since this dress put my hourglass shape on full display. My patent leather, snake-skinned Calvin Klein pumps and black snake-skinned Fendi bag really set things off on the outside, while my barely-there black stockings, Juicy Couture garter, thong, and demi-bra held my secrets beneath. Those secrets were mine for now, but would be used to my advantage by the end of the day.

Right when I hit the last step, Xavier glanced up, but he didn't make a move. I waited for a couple of seconds and then, I pulled open the door myself. I couldn't believe he didn't even come over to push the door open for me.

But after what I'd put him through, what could I expect?

He didn't even say hello. He just whispered, "Can I have a word with you?"

Now, while I had thought that our church was the best place to have this discussion, I was surprised that Xavier wanted to do this right here. I mean, folks would be walking in for the service and in just a few minutes, the lobby would be crowded with people standing around, greeting their friends, and waiting for their pew buddies. And even right now, there were more than enough stank folks standing to create an audience that would make our business theirs.

While pulling out my Handi-Wipes, I greeted him with a smile. "Good morning, Minister Xavier," I said, as I wiped my hands, needing to clean them after I'd touched that grimy door. "Can this wait until after service? I'm running late, and I refuse to dishonor Holy ground."

Now, you may think I was just throwing around a line or two, but I respected the house of the Lord and I had no intention of having this discussion until well after service. And, actually, I didn't want to talk in the church at all. I was hoping that we would have the talk in the parking lot so that our words would be between just the two of us. I especially didn't want the nosey old bats who were standing around included.

I expected Xavier to agree. Surely he didn't want to display our business in public. But then, he surprised me. He grabbed my arm and pulled me into an embrace. Just at that moment, the front door opened and Sister Stroman strolled in, with her Bible in her hand and her nose in the air. She was the First Lady, so you would have expected her to say something to somebody. But she just walked away like she was the most important person in the building. I smiled because she wasn't heading in the direction of the sanctuary. She was on her way to Malik's office.

Good! That meant that I would get to the sanctuary before she did and I'd be able to execute the first part of my plan without any problems from her. God's favor was shining on me already, but I wasn't surprised. Didn't the scriptures say that all things work together for good for those who love The Lord?

My attention returned to Xavier, though, when he hissed, "Listen to me, Sasha. I don't know what kind of games you're playing, but I've been here for you. I'm the man God intends to be your husband, not Pastor Stroman."

My eyebrows stretched to the top of my forehead. Really? Xavier thought that God wanted us to be together? While he'd often talked about us being a couple, he'd never talked about marriage. Well, now that I thought about it, maybe he had, but I never let him really talk about it since that discussion served no purpose.

But now, I realized that Xavier's thoughts about us was far worse than I thought and I felt bad. There was nothing I could do about it, though.

His lips hardly moved as he continued, "Don't you know he's a man of God who's happily married?" he said as if I didn't already know that. Well, I knew about the married part, but Malik was far from being happy. He couldn't be because if he were, God wouldn't have put together this plan.

But I guess Xavier didn't know all of that because he kept talking. "Pastor's certainly not going to leave his wife or lose his church over some little girl with a big crush."

He paused as if he expected me to say something, or come to my senses. I'm not sure which. But I said nothing, and I had more sense than he did at this moment. Because I was doing what God wanted.

Xavier said, "You actually want me to believe that God would ordain for you to take another woman's husband?"

Then, he shocked me for a second time when he leaned over and kissed me. A gentle, warm kiss that felt so sincere I almost felt bad. I closed my eyes and let his lips linger on mine. Now, I wasn't trying to lead him on, but it was just that Xavier's kisses were the best. Not that I had anyone to compare him to, but whenever he kissed me, I could feel it all the way down to my soul. Even now, standing in the church where I was about to become the First Lady, it was hard for me to break away because this felt so good, it almost felt right. And I enjoyed the familiarity of this connection. In that moment, I realized that I wasn't completely ready to let my best friend go.

But I couldn't get caught up like this. Especially not with Malik so close by. That's why I finally broke away, and then turned from him as if he nor the kiss mattered to me. I didn't get two steps away, though. Xavier gently grabbed my arm, pulled me back, and whispered in my ear, "Didn't you feel that? That's what you mean to me. I love you, Sasha, and I don't intend to stand back and watch you make a fool of yourself."

If he had just left it at loving me, it would've been a beautiful moment. But he'd had the audacity to call me a fool? With all the force I could muster, I whipped my hand right across his cheek. Honestly, I tried to slap the taste from his mouth, but I certainly slapped him hard enough so that he'd think about it before he ever called me a fool again.

As he stood there, recuperating more from embarrassment than pain, I stepped aside, not looking at him, and not looking at that audience of nosy biddies who stood there gaping as if they had front row tickets to some show.

When I walked into the sanctuary I pushed what had just happened between me and Xavier far from my mind. Instead, I allowed myself to be caught up in the majesty of this moment. Even though I'd been home from college for almost three weeks now, this was my first time back at Grace Tabernacle.

"Good to see you, Pink," one of the ushers said as he approached me.

I nodded, smiled and then followed him down the left-side aisle. I knew exactly where he was trying to lead me—I'd sat in the second row with my parents ever since I was a child. But when he stopped at the second pew, I moved right to the front.

"Pink," he whispered.

I just pretended I didn't hear him, which wasn't hard to do. The choir was up and in it.

"We've come this far by faith! Trusting in The Lord!"

They swayed and the congregation moved with them. So, when I didn't answer the usher, he just moved right back up the aisle to greet the next church member. Then, I sat down. Right in the front row, first seat, and I savored the feeling. I felt like I was sitting upon a throne rather than just on a fabric-covered pew. I had returned to Grace Tabernacle to claim everything that was mine, and that included this front row seat.

When the choir got to the second verse, I stood and sang and swayed with them. Closing my eyes, I worshipped God in all His reverence. On the outside, I sang. But inside, I prayed and thanked Him for my life—my future husband, my future children, and my future home.

After a few minutes, I couldn't even sing anymore. I was so full of gratitude for all that The Lord had given to me and was about to pour into my life. A tear slipped through my closed eye and rolled down my cheek, but I kept on worshiping. I had blocked out the world, keeping my mind just on my praise and worship.

Until I felt a tap on my shoulder. I couldn't imagine who would be rude enough to interrupt my time with God.

I opened my eyes and looked right into the eyes of Malik's wife, wondering what in the world did she want with me?

She stared me down and finally hissed, "Please move over."

At first, I just stood there because I really couldn't figure out what she was talking about. And then, I got it. I'd forgotten that I was sitting in what she thought was her seat. It was hers, technically. But one thing I knew about God was that He wanted us to claim what we wanted and I was claiming this seat. She needed to get used to seeing me here. I was absolutely sure that she already knew what was going to happen. God wouldn't have told me without telling her. She had to know that a change was coming and very soon, everything that had been hers would be mine. Well, not everything. I was going to have her man, her house, and this seat on the front pew, but her funny-looking clothes? She could keep all of those.

"I said, move over," she repeated as if that would mean anything to me. She waved her hand, gesturing for me to move to the left.

But just like the tree planted by the water in the Bible, I was not going to be moved. Wearing a graceful smile, I leaned in just a little. I didn't want to get too close and draw attention to her shameless Especially Yours outfit. I whispered, "I will not. I arrived on time for service, like you should have."

"Well, I've never…"

"Well, you just did." I turned back around in time to see Malik strutting into the pulpit, followed by Xavier, and two other ministers. It was only because I'd lost my focus that she was able to squeeze her fat ass beside me.

But right now, I didn't have time for his wife. I kept my eyes on Malik as he faced his seat on the altar, then, knelt down. When he bowed his head in prayer, my heart lurched, my nipples tingled, and my mouth watered. Just seeing him brought back the memory of last night when he'd kissed my cheek and sent a message to that spot between my legs. I watched him until he stood, and then, turned to face his people, and just seeing him standing there with all of that Godly power took my breath away.

That man was too fine for words. His rich, dark chocolate skin was so smooth, I wanted to reach out and caress him from my seat. In all his glory, Malik stood six-feet, two inches, just a few inches taller than my daddy.

Today, he wore a black robe with gold piping straight down the center. The sleeves were puffed and gold piping circled each one. He was wearing a gold linked bracelet and of course, his rock star smile.

Malik picked up his Bible and with his long, dark fingers, he flipped through the pages. I pretended the simple gold band on his left hand was platinum. With me, he would only wear the best. With her, I assumed it didn't matter.

My eyes stayed on his fingers and I imagined where he would touch me first. Would it be my face, or maybe my hips? Would his fingers start at my neck and travel the length of my body until he came in contact with the purest part of me—the special place I'd reserved just for him?

"Mmmm." The thought of how he would take me caused me to moan out loud. I hadn't meant to do that, but really, I didn't care.

"Humph."

I didn't care about that either. Malik's soon-to-be-ex could make all the disgusting sounds she wanted.

"Saints, turn with me in the Bible to John 3:16."

As he read, I watched his lips move and the way his chest rose and fell when he spoke about Jesus the Christ. I could feel Malik's love for God all the way in my seat. That was just one of the reasons why I already loved him. His love for God showed me how he would love me.

Then my daydream skidded to a halt.

"Good morning, Saints."

I folded my arms as Xavier stood at the pulpit. "This is the day the Lord has made, let us rejoice and be glad in it. God is good all the time." Of course Grace Tabernacle responded with a big, "and all the time, God is good." And then X went on, "Here at Grace we would like to extend to our visitors a warm and welcoming hello, so if you're here for the first time, please stand."

I twisted around just a bit so that I could see the thirty or so people who stood. As was the custom at our church, those sitting closest to the visitors greeted them.

Xavier said, "We want to thank you for visiting us today and if by chance you're seeking a church home, our doors and our hearts are always open."

The whole time he spoke to the congregation, X's eyes kept coming back to mine and each time, he wore his usual, what I called gangster smirk. Actually, he looked like he was about to burst out laughing—at me. I had no idea what he found so funny. Was it because I'd smacked him? Or did he find humor seeing me sitting next to Sister Stroman?

Whatever it was, I glared back at him, still upset that he'd called me a fool. Of course I'd expected him to be upset, but resorting to calling me names? That was so uncalled for and so unbecoming of the man of God that he was supposed to be.

As Xavier moved from greeting the visitors to making the church announcements, my anger began to fade. The more I thought about just how hard this had to be for Xavier. It had to be hard for him to give me up, just like it was hard for me to give him up. He really did mean a lot to me and I was going to miss him...and his kisses.

X was skilled, although as good as he was, I was sure that Malik would be better. And my love for Malik would be more complete, since I'd saved the most important part of myself for him.

"Pink!"

I blinked, a little embarrassed that I'd allowed my thoughts to wander like that while I was sitting so close to the altar. I looked up; Malik and Xavier stood side by side at the podium and Malik's arm was outstretched toward me.

Malik said, "Pink, would you come forward?"

Since my mind had been on...other things, I wasn't quite sure what had happened. Why had Malik called my name? Why did he want me to come up to the altar?

I almost didn't feel worthy to approach the altar at this moment, but in obedience, I stood, placed my clutch on the pew behind me, and slowly made my way to the front. The entire time, my eyes were on Malik, and his were on me. When I got to the two steps that led to the raised altar, he came down to hold my hand and help me up.

The moment we touched, a warm, tingling sensation filled me completely. The skin-to-skin contact was so electrifying, that I had to pull away. But Malik wouldn't let me go. The current that had just surged through me, had gone through him, too. I knew it by the way his eyes widened with surprise, then he shook himself as if he were trying to get rid of the feeling. I almost did a cartwheel right there. Malik didn't know what hit him.

My eyes were still locked on Malik's, but I could feel Xavier looking at me, too. Malik positioned me to his right and he stood between me and Xavier.

"Church," Malik started, "I've asked these two young people to join me here at the pulpit today because I want you all to know that I've chosen them to head our Singles' Ministry."

What? He wanted me to do what with Xavier?

There was light, polite applause.

When the congregation became quiet again, Malik said, "Let me tell you about these two young people. Some of you may remember Sister Sasha, or should I say, Sister Pink." He paused and then Malik's eyes roamed from my head to my four-inch stilettos that still didn't bring me close enough to his lips. "Yes, we call her Pink, for obvious reasons."

That little remark earned him a little praise from the brothers; there were chuckles of appreciation from the men. But from the sisters? Well, you know the deal.

He went on to say, "While Sister Pink was away at school, she began her own ministry on the campus of Spelman College, and then, along with Minister Xavier," he faced X before he turned back to me, "they began spreading the word of God through prayers sessions for the young folk at both of their schools."

Murmurs of approval rang through the sanctuary and I shifted from one leg to the other. It felt funny standing up here with Malik in front of the congregation. I mean, yes, I expected to be standing here next to him. I imagined that we would announce our relationship to everyone one Sunday morning after Malik began his divorce proceedings. I was ready for that, but I wasn't ready for this—here with Malik *and* Xavier. And the three of us standing together as Malik announced that he wanted me to work with Xavier. This didn't make sense. This wasn't right.

"I'm so proud of both of them," Malik continued, "and that's why I want them to take on this project together. Who better to replace Sister Sherita and Brother Charles!"

Amens and laughter rose through the congregation.

I frowned. What did everyone know that I didn't?

"Oh, Sister Pink," Malik said to me, but he was still facing the congregation. "You probably don't know this, but the Singles' Ministry has been led by Sister Sherita and Brother Charles for the last four years. And they've done a wonderful job. So wonderful that the two of them married...and they're right now, on their honeymoon in Jamaica."

"Amen!" someone shouted.

"And who knows," Malik said, looking from me to Xavier. He didn't have to say anything else. I got the message.

Ugh! I was ready to kill myself. No wonder X had been wearing that silly smirk when he greeted the visitors. Malik had probably told him about this before they entered the sanctuary. Well, if he thought for one minute that I would be heading any ministry with him, he was sadly mistaken. By the time I finished my plan with Malik, he would pull me away from Malik and the Singles' Ministry so fast...he wouldn't want me anywhere near Xavier. In fact, I wouldn't be surprised if when we were finally together, Malik asked Xavier to leave the church. Maybe Xavier would move back to Atlanta. Surely, he could find a position in some church there.

So talking about grinning and bearing it, I just continued to stand there, smiling and upholding my princess stature. I was way too sharp to let this little situation raise my temperature. The only time I wanted to feel my temperature rising was in the bedroom with Malik.

"So for all of you singles, I've decided to keep the ministry going straight through the summer under the leadership of these two amazing young singles. So put this on your calendar, in your phone, on your iPads, or in whatever gadget you have...."

Laughter and "Amen!" shouts came from the parishioners.

Malik said, "The first Singles' meeting will be held on not this Saturday, but the following Saturday, June 15 at three o'clock. Amen?"

"Amen," the congregation agreed.

People were still clapping as I walked back to my seat. After I'd taken just a few steps, I noticed my clutch on the floor. Seemed like Sister Stroman had needed the extra room to slide her wide hips into the space where I'd been sitting.

It only took me a split second to decide that I was going to make her regret the moment when she'd touched my belongings. She'd never do it again.

Slowly, I turned around, faced the altar and said, "Thank you, Pastor, for giving me this opportunity."

He nodded with a smile. "You're most welcome, Sister Pink."

I knew his eyes were still on me when I turned my back to him, bent over, retrieved my purse, and then took my time standing upright once again.

Yep, I gave him and everyone else behind me a reason to blush.

When I looked back to the altar, Malik's eyes were almost glazed over, and I imagined him moaning, "Mmmm, mmmm, mmmm." Of course, he didn't do that. He was in church. He was a man of God and way too classy to do anything like that. But I could tell what was going on in his mind. He was doing everything that he could to keep his lust in check.

His reaction was pleasing enough, but then, when I scanned my surroundings, I wanted to lift my hands and shout Hallelujah. Gone was Xavier's grin. Gone was Sister Stroman's smirk. Yes! The collateral damage was even better.

Taking my time, I sat and wiggled my butt until I was totally comfortable in the seat.

For the rest of the service, I smiled, though I couldn't say the same for Xavier and Sister Stroman. The two of them wore matching frowns and I was sure at any moment one or both of them would growl. I wanted to burst out laughing. That's what they got for messing with me.

As Malik preached from the book of John, he talked about how God loved us so much that He sent His son Jesus to save us. "Saints I'm telling you that God loves us unconditionally.

He wants the best for us. He wants us to live in the fullness of His love and He wants us to love one another."

It was amazing that this was the scripture Malik was preaching from on my very first time at back Grace Tabernacle. John 3:16 was one of the scriptures that God had given to me as He spoke to my heart about me and Malik. I guess I really shouldn't have been surprised. It was all working together for the good that God wanted in my life.

As Malik preached and strutted on the altar, I once again, let my mind wander, this time to what it would be like being the First Lady? I was young and this church was used to having women who were almost ancient. That was one blessing I was going to bring to the church—my youth, my vitality, my young and fresh sensibilities.

Then, I wondered about where would we live? Because I certainly wasn't going to be in any house where his wife had lived. I wondered if we would live in DC or maybe in Montgomery County in Maryland or Fairfax County in Virginia. Yes, maybe Fairfax—there were many upscale communities with great school systems. And the school systems would be important for our children. I'd want to wait a couple of years, but then, we would have two—one of each. A boy who would look just like Malik and a little girl, a mini me who I would dress in pink and patent leather the way my mom had dressed me. The only difference—my daughter and I would wear matching outfits. Yes, we would be quite a family.

Suddenly, I felt Sister Stroman move and all around me the congregants stood. Was it time for the benediction already? Had I daydreamed through the rest of the sermon and the invitation?

I bowed my head as Malik gave the benediction, then, looked up with everyone else. When I did, Malik's eyes were already on me.

"Sister Pink?" he called and waved me over at the same time.

This was the point where Malik usually greeted the members and visitors, but I guess his mind was just on me today.

With my clutch in my hand this time, I sauntered toward the pastor and watched his eyes take a slow Sunday stroll over every inch of my body.

"Yes, Pastor?"

"I...I...I...."

Boyaah! He could hardly talk because of me.

He cleared his throat and then continued, "I would like for you and Minister Xavier to make your way to my office and perhaps do a little brainstorming so that we can be ready for the first Single's gathering since I didn't give you that much time to plan." He had to pause and clear his throat once again.

The last thing I wanted was to be anywhere with Xavier. But once again, I was going to show Malik that I was ready to be an obedient wife.

"Like I told the church," Malik continued, "the two of you are the Saints who will get this done and done well."

As I stood there and watched Malik's plump lips move, a plan began to form in my head. I knew exactly how I was going to get Malik to my home and in my bed. As he talked, I calculated all of my next steps.

"Thank you, Pastor," Xavier said.

"Yes, thank you," I added. "And, I won't let you down."

The way I batted my eyelashes at him, and then the way he took a deep breath, I knew he understood that my words meant so much more. He knew I wasn't just talking about this Singles' Ministry.

Xavier must've seen and felt what was going on between me and Malik because he stepped between us as if he really had a chance at blocking and stopping the inevitable. Xavier extended his hand to me, and at first, I hesitated. But then, with all eyes on me I took his hand. I had to play my role, be the good girl, and so, X and I walked together from the sanctuary and into the hall that led to the administrative offices.

But once we were out of sight, Xavier dropped my hand like it was a snake, and he grabbed my arm instead. In the lobby, he'd grabbed me, too, as he pulled me into an embrace, and I needed him to break this habit that he seemed to be forming. He needed to take his hands off of me.

But even though I wiggled and squirmed, X wouldn't allow me to shake free.

"Let me..." Before I could complete my sentence, Xavier opened the door to the pastor's office and practically threw me inside. "Hey, watch it!" I exclaimed, stumbling just a little bit.

It was as if Xavier didn't even hear me. He went straight into his own rant. "Do you know how many times I called you last night?" he said, picking up from the argument we'd had in the lobby.

I folded my arms, not saying a word. I knew how many times he'd called by the dozens of messages he'd left.

He continued as if I needed a specific number. "A million times, Pink! I called you all night because I was hoping that we could talk and I could get you to see just how ridiculous you're being."

"You need to check your language with me," I snapped. "First, you call me a fool, and now, you're saying that I'm ridiculous?" I released a bitter chuckle. "That's not the way to convince me of anything."

He held up his hands and calmed down a little. "I'm sorry. I'm not trying to hurt you, but I don't know any other way to say this because you're not listening. I know you know God's Word. I know you know that He would never ordain you taking another woman's husband."

Really, I was sick of talking to Xavier about this, but for right now, I had to keep this conversation going. We had to talk long enough for Malik to come back to his office. And then, the show would be on!

"You're so much better than this," Xavier said softly. "Talk to me." He reached for me once again; this time, he grasped my arm gently.

The last thing I needed was for Xavier to calm down. I needed all of his rage and fury in full effect. So, I mustered up a little base in my voice and turned my volume up. I yanked my arm away from him as if he'd just committed a major offense. "Get your hands off of me!"

He backed up, a little, as if he was surprised by my reaction. As he moved, I stepped closer to the door. This was an old building and I knew I'd be able to hear Malik coming toward his office once he finished with the church members.

Xavier's eyes were on me when I leaned against the door looking weary as if all of this exhausted me. "Look, X," I began with a sigh, "I always told you that we could never be more than friends." I paused, making sure that my ears were open to the sounds in the hallway.

Continuing, I said, "I really did hear, God. I know you don't believe me and you think that I'm a fool, and ridiculous. But when I told Malik...."

His eyes got so wide. "Hold up! You told Pastor that?"

I shook my head. "Not directly. I did tell him that I was saving myself, but I didn't have to say anything else because I was sure that God had told him, too."

Xavier shook his head slowly as if he really felt sorry for me. "You know that doesn't make sense, right?"

"Well, aren't you the one who always says that if it doesn't make sense, it's probably God?"

"Yes, but I wasn't talking about confusion. God's not the author of confusion. And God saying that you should be with a married man is nothing but confusion and nonsense."

Xavier needed to back up with all of this name calling. First I was a fool, then I was being ridiculous, and now what God had told me was nonsense? If Xavier wasn't part of this plan, if I didn't need him in this moment, I would just walk out the door.

But right now, even though he didn't know it, Xavier was my co-star and I needed him to play his part.

I said, "The Pharisees called Jesus foolish, too."

He leaned back a little. "Oh, so now, you're comparing yourself to Jesus?"

"No, of course I'm not doing that," I said, wanting to punch him in his face and then, stomp out of the room. But, I stood my ground for my greater purpose. "All I know is that there are many things that Christians say and do and other people look upon them as foolish. And I'm not the first one that this has happened to. Remember that pastor on that reality show? God told him to leave his wife and marry someone else. And he was obedient."

"Yup, and he ended up on a reality show with half the congregation he used to have because God hadn't told him that."

"How do you know what God told him? How do you know what God told me?" But then, I held up my hand, stopping him from saying anything. "Look, Xavier," I said with a sigh, "you're my best friend and I was really hoping we could remain that way. But if you feel like we can't be friends, then we won't. Just so you know, for the record, I have always cherished our friendship and I would hate for it to end just because I was walking the path that God has set for me."

X stepped closer and this time, he gently placed both of his hands on my shoulders. "From the bottom of my heart, I believe that the path God has set for you is with me."

I felt myself blinking rapidly. That was the second time that Xavier had said this.

He continued, "That's what God told me. He told me that you were going to be my wife and if you would just give all of this up, I know that I can make you happy."

His words were so gentle, so kind, and almost believable. If God hadn't already chosen my mate, I would've had to give Xavier serious consideration.

But then, he just had to add, "Just drop all this foolishness and realize that the man that God is talking to you about is me."

Xavier reached up as if he were about to give me a hug. Not that I would've hugged him. Especially since he'd called me foolish once again. But outside, I heard footsteps coming toward the door and I prayed that they were Malik or else I was about to waste a great performance and someone was about to get a great show.

Just as the door opened, I placed my hands on Xavier's chest, shoved him away, turned on the waterworks, and screamed, "I don't want a relationship with you. I told you what God said to me, and you of all people should know how much He orders my steps."

"What is going on here?" Malik asked.

This was the perfect scene. The only thing—I wish I hadn't pushed Xavier away. It would've been better if his hands were on me. But my tears, and the way I was trembling were good enough.

I shook my head and lowered it, making sure that tears dripped from my eyes.

"Sister Pink, what is going on?"

His eyes were still moving between me and Xavier and finally X motioned toward me with his hands.

"Go ahead Pink," Xavier challenged me, "tell him what you just told me."

If X thought that I was intimidated or afraid to tell Malik what was going on, he was mistaken and sadly so. But, I wasn't going to jump through hoops just because Xavier told me to. Plus, it was part of my plan to keep my mouth shut, at least for now.

"Sister Pink?"

That was my cue. With my tears still falling and my head still shaking, I turned toward the opened door and ran. I was sure that Malik would come after me; I just didn't know if it would be now or later. Not that it really mattered—either way, I was going to see him. And when I did, I was going to be one hundred percent ready.

Chapter 4

I tried to keep within the speed limit on my way home. There was no need for me to be stopped by the police. Sure, I could talk myself out of getting any ticket. But being stopped would've slowed me down and I didn't need any delays. I had to get home and get ready.

It was hard to keep my excitement down, though. I was thrilled with my performance, which had been standing-ovation perfect. Malik had found me distraught, without explanation. Even when I ran from his office, my acting continued. He'd called my name several times, but I just kept running, never looking back. It was the way he called my name, with such urgency, that let me know that I was right— he would be coming after me.

My prayer was that only Malik would come, and not Xavier. Hopefully my act had made Xavier so mad he was ready to be done with me. But I hoped he wasn't so done that he'd tell Malik what I'd shared with him. Not that I really thought he would. Xavier cared for me too much to betray my confidence. When Malik asked him what was wrong, he'd probably just say that he had no idea why I was crying. Or maybe he would say it must be a woman thing.

Whatever, it would be enough to insure that Malik would be on his way to my place. He knew where I lived since I'd sent out announcements about moving into my condo and just last week I'd received a congratulatory card back from Malik and his wife. I'd sent the card just to signal to Malik that I was back. I didn't have any idea that it was going to play out that he would need my address, and this soon.

Rolling my car into the undercover garage, the tires screeched as I took a couple of the turns faster than the 5 MPH posted signs. I parked, jumped out, and then as I rode up in the elevator, I thought about what I was about to do.

Presentation was everything. So, should I strip down to my underwear or would one of my naughty negligees be better?

By the time I rushed into my condo, I decided that I would strip down to my underwear and then, just cover up with my pink baby-doll robe. It was short, way short. And to give it a little extra sexy-fabulous kick, I'd leave on the garter and the stockings that I wore to church.

Still moving quickly, I dashed into the bathroom. Checking my reflection in the mirror, my make-up was still fresh and perfect—almost. I cleaned up my mascara and then, did a little smoky eye with my black pencil. Next, came my hair. I pulled my tresses up and into a long ponytail.

Another glance in the mirror, a quick spray of Pink Jeans by Versace behind my ears and on my wrists, and then, just as I slid back into my stilettos, my telephone rang.

"Ms. Jansen," the concierge in my building said, "you have a visitor."

I held my breath. "Who is it?" I asked, praying that I'd been right. Praying that Xavier was too angry to come, and Malik cared so much he had to come.

The concierge said, "Pastor Malik Stroman."

"Thank-you," I exhaled. "Send him right up, please."

When I hung up, I wanted to dance, but there was no time for celebration. Instead, I used the time to reflect on this journey that I'd taken and how God was about to give me all the desires of my heart. This was what I'd been waiting for my entire life. Okay, maybe that was a slight exaggeration, but at my age, six years felt like a lifetime.

My heart took a few extra beats, but then when I heard the soft knock on the door, my heart was set at ease.

My love had arrived.

I only had a couple of seconds, but I quickly kneeled before my sofa, closed my eyes and prayed, "Thank you, Father, for this blessing." I pushed myself up, smoothed down my robe, then strutted to the door.

His eyes widened just a little when I opened the door. For extra effect, I put one hand on my hip. Malik cleared his throat and I wanted to jump up and down, clap my hands, and do one of those Brazilian Zumba moves.

"Sister Pink." His voice sounded like he was weak.

My grin was so wide, but then, I heard my name again, "Sister Pink," and it wasn't Malik's voice.

Malik stepped aside, and his wife moved in front of him. My mouth fell wide open. *What in the world?*

"May we come in?" Malik asked the question, but that woman didn't wait for an answer. She marched past me, leaving a trail of her cheap perfume. She paused for a second to look me up and down, then, she continued moving as if she had an invitation, which, of course, she did not.

I was too shocked to speak, though I did my best to keep my game face on. By the time I stepped aside so that Malik could come in, his wife was already sitting on my suede sofa.

As Malik sat next to his wife, I didn't know whether to tell her to get out or to ask Malik if he'd lost his mind. I was still standing by the door when I faced them, not knowing what to say, not knowing what to do. But the way they both stared at me made me pull the edges of my robe together, trying to cover up just a little bit.

Malik's wife scrunched up her nose when she said to me, "Sister Pink, I know you weren't expecting company, but maybe you should go and cover up a bit more."

I glared at her. She was basically an intruder in my house, wearing some cheap cologne that would take me weeks to dispense of the stench that was sure to seep into my sofa. And now, she was talking to me as if she had a right? And, she was trying to give me etiquette lessons on the proper way I should dress in my home? This lady probably walked around in some thick, flannel robe with bunny slippers. She had no style, she had no class, and she had no business telling me what to do.

Still, I couldn't say that I felt comfortable standing there half-naked. Not that I was ashamed of my body in any way, but all of this was for Malik's eyes only. And as his future wife, I had to be mindful of how I presented myself in front of others.

I gave a little nod. "Excuse me; I'll be right back." I did an about face, and I knew their eyes were on me. So, I added just a little swing in my step—that was meant for both of them.

But once I closed my bedroom door, I wanted to scream. And I did—in my head. That battle-axe! Freakin' Broomhilda! Damn Fiona! What was she doing here? Why had she come? But the most important question—why had Malik let her come? This was supposed to be our time, Malik knew that. I was tired of waiting and I wanted what was supposed to be mine.

I was fuming as I picked out my pink Victoria's Secret jogging suit from my closet. By the time I slipped into my clothes and glanced at myself in the mirror, I had calmed down. I may have been covered up, but with the way these sweat pants hugged my booty, I might as well have been naked. And with the word 'Pink' spread from one end of my butt to the other, if I turned around, I knew exactly where Malik's eyes would be. When I slipped into the jacket, I left it unzipped on purpose. The tiny pink tee I wore was fitted and put my young globes on full display. Now, whether I was coming or going, Malik was going to be one happy man.

I sauntered out of my bedroom, but then stopped shy of the kitchen. I had a great view of that woman snooping through my house! Well, maybe snooping was a strong word, but she was certainly checking out my possessions.

Malik sat on my sofa with his eyebrows drawn together and his hands clasped. I could tell he didn't approve, but he didn't say anything as his wife picked up my pink Waterford praying hands. I wanted to rush over to her and snatch that precious ornament away from her. It was a one-of-a-kind piece that my father had commissioned from the Waterford company because they hadn't manufactured any items in pink. But at my father's request, and I'm sure for a hefty price, he'd had that made for me.

Finally, she returned the ornament to the shelf on my étagère, then she paused and took notice of my framed degree that hung just above the Victorian glass table my mother had purchased for me as a house-warming gift. When Malik's wife ran her finger across the ivory china frame that held my diploma, I decided that it was time to put a stop to all of this.

But just before I stepped into the living room, my eyes moved to Malik and that made me pause. He was looking directly at me. I smiled, and he did, too. With my smile still in place, I nodded slightly, and raised one eyebrow as I looked at where his wife was still moving around my home.

He shrugged his shoulders in an apologetic manner and that move made me love him and feel sorry for him at the same time. It wasn't his fault that he had a wife who was so uncoothed. He wouldn't have to worry about that for long. His next wife had nothing but class.

"Okay, I'm ready," I said, finally revealing myself to both of them.

When she turned around, Malik's wife took notice of me once again, looking me over just like she'd done before.

"Let's sit down," I said, determined to remain gracious. Even though all I wanted to do was kick her out, I would never be disrespectful. I'd been raised too well for that kind of behavior. Don't get it twisted, though. I didn't respect her, I just knew how to be civil.

She returned to her spot beside Malik, while I sat on a soft cushioned over-sized chair that was directly across from them. I crossed my legs, yoga-style (showing off, I know.) Then, I smiled, but said nothing as I waited for one of them to tell me why they were there. Well, I knew what Malik wanted, but unless he'd brought his wife to watch...I just couldn't imagine what this meeting was about.

"Sister Pink..."

I guess she was going to be the spokesperson.

She said, "Pastor and I thought maybe it was time for us all to get together and have a little talk."

"About what?" I asked, frowning.

She turned to her husband. "I'm going to let him take it from here since he has a much better understanding of what's been going on."

I shrugged and nodded and turned to Malik.

He cleared his throat before he stood. Then, he took steps toward me.

I had to stop the smile from spreading across my face as he came closer to me. Whether he'd made that move on purpose or he'd just come closer because he was drawn to me, I didn't know. Now, he was so close that I could smell the manly fragrance of his woody cologne. But it wasn't his cologne that had my attention. It was the bulge in his pants that made me sit up straight. Maybe that's why he had to stand and get away from his wife. Maybe he wanted to make sure that she didn't see it.

I wondered what was it about me that had turned him on? Was it the way I'd met him at the door? Or did he prefer me to be covered up so that his imagination could go wild? Whatever the reason, him and his bulge had just made me very happy.

But then, he kneeled in front of me, took my hand, and I frowned. What was he getting ready to do? And was he really going to do this in front of his wife?

My heart pounded as Malik began, "Sister Pink, a few years ago I kind of felt as though maybe you had a little crush on me."

A crush? Why was he belittling my feelings like that?

He continued, "When you whispered in my ear during the purity ceremony, I was taken aback. When I went home and told my wife about it," he paused for a moment and looked over...at *her,* "we laughed about it. It was cute, clearly it was just an infatuation."

An infatuation? Was he kidding? How could something that came from God be an infatuation?

I let Malik keep on without interruption. "Infatuations happen," he said. "When there's an older man that you hold in high regard, maybe you see him as a father figure or a teacher..."

A father figure? First of all, he was way too young for me to consider him a father to anyone besides the children that he and I would have together. And, I didn't have any kind of Oedipus Complex, something that I had studied in my Psych 101 class when I was a freshman.

But I wasn't going to get into all of this with Malik. So, I just pressed my lips together, determined not to say a word and just as determined to not let his words faze me. Though I had to admit, I was a little shaken. I couldn't tell if Malik really believed what he was saying, or was it just a show for her?

When I glanced at Sister Stroman, I knew for sure that this was just a show. If given a choice, there was no way Malik would prefer this homely woman who wasn't even stylish enough to color the graying edges of her hair. Malik, and every other man would always choose me, so clearly, he was just saying this because she was here. He probably hadn't figured out yet how he was going to handle how to get rid of her.

If it were me, I would just come straight out and tell her that she had to go. But, I had to respect Malik for the way he wanted to do it. He was such a gentle and kind man; he probably wanted to let her down easy.

"Whatever it is," Malik continued, breaking me out of my thoughts, "we know it's just a phase that you're going through."

I raised an eyebrow. He was taking this act a little too far.

He said, "When you went off to school, and started writing me, I wanted to support and guide you as your pastor. That's why I sent you the study guides and the other materials, and that's why I introduced you to Xavier. I wasn't being a matchmaker, I just wanted to steer you in the direction of someone who was your own age."

Our eyes were locked together when I heard, "Malik!"

Her squeaky voice broke our trance and he stood, then returned to where he'd been sitting. That surprised me. He was behaving as if she was the one in charge.

When he sat down, she gave me this big ole grin. Like she had just won a prize or something. Really? Did she not realize that she could never compete with me. Did she not know that she had no chance of winning?

She said, "Pastor told me about the discussion that you had with Xavier after the services today."

Shut up! I screamed inside my head. I was really trying hard to be the young woman that my parents raised me to be. But on the other side of being pissed, I was really surprised. Had Xavier really told Malik what I'd said? How much had he told him and how did Malik feel now? I didn't want to hear his words from the script that he'd prepared for his wife. I wanted to hear the words that were in his heart.

But Sister Stroman kept talking, not giving Malik a chance to say a word. She said, "And from what Pastor overheard," she paused and looked at him. When he nodded, she continued, "It seems like you may have another agenda."

You don't get to talk to me about this! I said inside. On the outside, I stayed quiet.

Sister Stroman continued, "Sister Pink, you're a young Christian woman who has so much going for her."

At least she recognized that.

As if they were a tag team, Malik picked it up from there, "I'm flattered, Sister Pink. It's not often that an old man like me gets noticed anymore."

The pastor and his wife chuckled, but I didn't find anything funny.

Malik said, "But we came over here today to make sure that you know that I can't condone nor reciprocate any feelings you may have for me. As a pastor, a husband, and a man of God, I walk my talk. What I preach and what I teach is how

I live my life. I will always be true to my Lord and Savior, as well as myself."

Oh, please! If he were being true, then he would be with me. He would follow God and not be distracted by this mistake of a marriage.

Malik said, "We just believe that once you get settled back in your life here in D.C., God will bring a wonderful young man to you."

Yeah, right! If he believed a word he was saying, then why were his eyes continuing to wander and settle on my exposed cleavage?

"Like my wife said, you're a wonderful Christian woman who has the love of Christ in her heart..."

Blah, blah, blah. I was so tired of listening to this corny crap. Then, he said, "And who knows what can happen with you and Minister Xavier? He might be the one."

I wanted to yawn out loud. Why wouldn't Malik just be honest? If he wanted to talk about right, he was the right man. Everything about him was right for me: the right pedigree, the right career, the right money. Even his height and complexion were right. He was the man who was in my dreams when I was a little girl. The man that I'd always imagined that I'd marry one day.

"Is there anything that you want to say, Sister Pink?" he asked me.

I let my glance lock on his for a moment, then, I looked at his wife. "No," I said. "I think the two of you have said enough."

That victorious smirk was back on her face as Malik and his wife stood. I wanted to tell her to look down between her husband's legs. I wanted to ask her which one of us was the reason why he had to keep straightening out his pants?

Pastor Malik walked back over to me and took my hand, urging me to stand. Once I stood, Sister Stroman clasped her hand into my free one and I had to fight what my mind was telling me to do—to snatch my hand away from hers.

Malik said, "Your parents have done a wonderful job of raising you into the perfect princess, Sister Pink. So, wait for your prince; wait on the Lord." I did my best not to roll my eyes. "There is a scripture, that I'm sure you know, Sister Pink. Where two or three are gathered in my name, I will be in the midst. So, since were joined here today, the three of us, let us pray."

Okay, now I had to work really hard not to laugh. So, I quickly lowered my head and closed my eyes as if I was going along with this facade. It was ridiculous, but until I could figure out my next steps, I had to go with this flow.

"Father God we come to you with praise and thanksgiving..."

I was surprised when Malik let his wife lead the prayer. I kept my head bowed and eyes shut for as long as I could... about ten seconds or so and then, I opened my eyes.

Both of their eyes were squeezed tightly, as if they weren't even going to let a sliver of light in. Looking down to where Malik held my hand, I squeezed his fingers, and just like that, he opened his eyes. I gave him a coy smile, and then watched him take a couple of quick breaths.

"We thank you for all of this, Father God...."

As his wife continued to pray, Malik stared at me and in his eyes, I could see everything. I could see that he wanted to know, that he wanted to try, that he wanted me.

"All this we ask in your precious Son's, Jesus' name... Amen!"

By the time Sister Stroman said, "Amen," she had no idea that she had just put the final seal on Malik and my fate.

"Sister Pink," she began in a tone that was strong and confident, "I know that The Lord is going to help you through. He is going to give you a bright future. And this little thing with my husband will be a thing of the past."

She said that like she believed it. As if she really believed that she was safe from me. I had no idea why her little prayer hadn't revealed the truth to her. With the way Malik had just looked at me, I knew that he was still trying to fight it, but he would give up soon. He was going to be mine, all mine.

"Have a good evening." Malik's words were like honey, so smooth, so sweet and I wondered if she noticed the change in his tone.

There was nothing for me to say as Sister Stroman led the way to the door. Malik followed closely behind her, and I followed closely behind him. She was so eager to leave that she didn't even wait for Malik to open the door. She just marched right out while Malik's steps were more hesitant. He slowed down as if he wanted to stay.

When he was just about to step over the threshold, I leaned against the door and whispered, "Goodnight, Malik."

He turned around, faced me, and this time, he did smile. This time, his eyes were bright, without questions. This time, he looked like he understood it all.

"Goodnight, Sister Pink," he said. And then, his eyes did one last slow stroll up and down my body.

I stuck out my chest so that he could have a better view and his stare sent all kinds of chills through me.

When he finally turned around, I slowly closed the door, then walked over to the sofa. I sat on the end where Malik had sat and imagined him here with me, without his wife. But he had shown up with her and what that showed me was that Malik was a faithful man. He had probably never even cheated on his wife, which made me love him all the more.

But what he had to realize was that what was going to happen between me and him would not be cheating. This would be consummating the inevitable. Thinking about the way he looked at me when he left, made me smile. It was just a matter of time now. All I had to do was help Malik to move forward.

It was time for Plan B.

Chapter 5

I woke up Monday morning completely ready. Since last night, I'd been planning, plotting and praying and I was ready to take this to the next level.

After I finished my morning prayer, I turned on my CD player and pressed the keys to get to my favorite song.

"Love is patient caring, love is kind. Love is best when it's genuine...."

As Hezekiah sang about the favor of God, I walked into my closet trying to determine what I would wear to the office. I hated that I even had to go in, but I had some pending proposals on my desk that couldn't wait and since I was a Bible believing woman and the Bible teaches to "give unto Caesar what is Caesar's," I had to focus on work and put my plan on hold for a few hours.

I pulled out my navy blue Christian Dior pencil skirt and blazer and decided to pair it up with a very classy multi-colored Dolce & Gabana halter. The weather app on my phone showed that today was going to be one of those almost 90 degree days and I wanted to stay cool. So this top was perfect.

I splashed a little Burberry Brit before I slipped into my multicolored, red bottom stilettos. I clicked off the CD player, then grabbed my Louis Vuitton briefcase. Of course, the colors of LV threw off my entire outfit, but I didn't care. My briefcase was a graduation gift from my brother, Joseph, and it was my favorite bag to carry to work.

From the time I stepped out of my apartment, got into the elevator, then slipped behind the wheel of my car, my mind was on Malik. Of course it was? What else was there to think about? That's all I'd done from the moment he and his wife had left my apartment yesterday afternoon. I thought about Malik and what our future would be like. I had it all planned out—how we would shop for a ring, how we would plan the gala that was going to be our wedding. Where we'd honeymoon, and then how we would begin looking for our own house when we got back from our fourteen wonderful days in Dubai, which is where I'd always dreamed of going for my honeymoon. Or maybe we would buy our home first, so that our place would be ready for us to move in when we returned from Dubai.

By the time I parked my car in the underground garage of my office building, I felt like I had every important moment of Malik's and my future planned out. As I took the elevator up to my office, my thoughts shifted a little. While I loved my position here at the magazine, I wondered what it would be like to just simply be a housewife. As ambitious as I was, being a wife and mother was what I really wanted. I wanted to stay at home so that my complete focus would be on Malik, and later on him and our children.

I guess I wanted to be like my mother, who never had to worry about how well she was doing on her job, or if the boss's daughter would return from New Zealand and replace her simply because she was the boss's daughter.

Not that I had those kinds of worries. Even though I'd just started, I knew I was doing well here at the magazine. And even if I weren't, I didn't have to worry. I was blessed to be from three generations of money—my great grandfather, who was born at the turn of the twentieth century, was one of the first African Americans to be appointed as an Appellate Court Judge in the 1940's. His son, my grandfather, followed in his footsteps, as did my father. But while they did make very good money as attorneys, the bulk of their fortune came from real estate. Back in the 1940's, my great grandfather began buying up real estate in Washington, DC. My grandfather continued the tradition, though he expanded into Maryland. And then there was my father who had taken the investment game to a whole 'nother level. My dad bought commercial real estate in the DMV that he flipped quickly for a profit. Now, the Jansens had a growing fortune that would provide for many generations to come.

I wasn't interested in living on my father's money, though. My parents would always be there if I needed them. But that wasn't necessary since Malik was more than capable of taking care of me.

Stepping off the elevator, I immediately walked into the hustle and bustle of the Power Play offices. There was a mass of cubicles, occupied by the secretaries, and a few of the copy editors that were on this floor. The chatter, the energy sent me straight into work-mode. I was ready to get to it as I strutted to my office.

Passing all the cubicles, I once again marveled at just how lucky, no, how blessed I was. I was a junior editor, so of course, I should have only had a cubicle. But because I had worked with Power Play in their Atlanta offices for the three summers that I was in school, I'd been given an office, to the chagrin of the three other junior editors who had been hired with me in May—as if I cared about them.

"Hey, girl," Amber, my secretary, called out to me as I approached her cubicle.

I gave her a long glare before I turned into my office. I knew Amber would be right behind me.

"I know, I know," she said as she followed me. She closed the door behind us. "I'm sorry," she apologized.

I was always correcting her and she was always apologizing. "Amber, you know that you can't talk to me like that out there."

"I said I was sorry," she huffed as she dropped into the chair in front of my desk. "From now on, I'll just say, 'Hello, Ms. Jansen'."

As I dropped my bag onto my desk, I shook my head, then took in the red dress that Amber was wearing. She was always sharp, but that silk red wrap with the turn-up collar was one of the flyest outfits I'd ever seen her wear.

"So," she continued, "are we still friends?"

"We'll always be friends, Amber. It's just that I don't want everyone out there to know it. You know those women already don't like me."

She waved her hand in the air. "So what? Even if you didn't help me get this job they wouldn't like you. So you might as well just go with the flow."

She was right about that. I'd never been friends with girls, so I never made friends with women. In fact, Amber was the only woman that I could come close to calling a friend. We'd been pretty close up until the third grade when my parents took me out of public school and sent me to the prestigious Sidwell Friends School. But because Amber and her parents attended Grace Tabernacle, I saw her every week.

While I went to Spelman, Amber had gone straight to work after high school. I hadn't seen her for four years, but my first day back, she'd called, taken me out to lunch, and told me she hated the health club where she'd been working. She'd been looking for a more professional job and since she was the only person I could call a friend, I used my feminine wiles, flirted with one of the guys in HR, and ten days after I started at *Power Play*, I had a new secretary.

"So," Amber said, interrupting my thoughts, "how was your weekend? You do anything special?"

The weekend. It had just been two days, but so much had happened. The anniversary dinner, the church service, and then, the visit. But all I said to Amber was, "It was okay."

She frowned as if she were waiting for more. When I didn't add anything, she asked, "So, you didn't hang out with that fine Xavier?"

I shook my head. I had never let Amber in on anything— not my relationship with Xavier, not what God had told me about Malik, nothing. We weren't girls like that. The only reason she even knew about Xavier was that he always called me here and twice he'd stopped by, making me have to explain a little to Amber. I'd told her that we were just friends from Atlanta, but she didn't believe me. She assumed that X was 'hitting it' as she liked to say.

"So you didn't see him over the weekend?" Amber pressed me.

Again, I just shook my head.

"Then, why has he been blowing up your phone all morning?" she asked.

I raised an eyebrow.

"Yup." She nodded. "After the third call, I stopped answering and let his calls go to your voicemail. So, I know you probably have a million messages on there from him."

I sighed. I knew this had been too good to be true. Since I'd run out of Malik's office yesterday, I hadn't heard a peep from Xavier. I just figured that he was finally done with me, though I can't say that I'd felt good about that.

But it looked like he wasn't done. It looked like he wasn't about to let anything go. It looked like I was going to have to deal with this.

"So if you and Xavier are just friends, why is he blowing up your phone?" Amber didn't even blink when she asked me that question. She asked like she had a right to know. But she should've known that if I hadn't said anything by now, it wasn't going to happen. My father had always told me that you couldn't share your dreams with just anyone. And with the way things had gone down with X, my daddy was right.

The way Amber sat—like she had no plans on ever moving—let me know that I was going to have to at least toss her a bone.

"Okay, I did see him," I said.

"Yes!" Amber said, pumping her fist in the air as if my words gave her some kind of victory.

"I saw him at church."

Her smile fell as fast as her fist. "What? Church?"

I nodded. "Yes, and Pastor asked Xavier and I to head the Singles Ministry. So, I suppose X is calling because he wants to go over the specifics and make some plans."

I nearly laughed out loud when she rolled her eyes. She wasn't even trying to hide the fact that she didn't believe me. "Mmm-hmm, I bet. That man thought I was lying when I told him you hadn't arrived yet. And his tone didn't sound like he wanted to talk about anything that had to do with church. Now, if you ask me…"

"That's just it, I haven't asked you!"

"Well, I guess that's my signal to get back to work," she said as if she had an attitude. But then when she stood up, she grinned. "But this isn't over. I'm gonna be right back in this chair after your meeting."

"What meeting?" I asked, clicking on the calendar icon on my iPad. "I don't have any meetings scheduled for today."

"That's what you think," she said right before she opened the door.

And standing there on the opposite side, looking as fine as he wanted to, was Xavier. As he stepped in, Amber stepped out, but she turned back and said, "You can thank me later." Then, she winked and closed the door.

In the silence of my office, Xavier stared at me and I stared at him. And then, he shifted from one foot to the other and I shifted in my chair. After a couple of seconds, he took a couple of steps and sat where Amber had been sitting. He sat as if he'd been invited to do so.

And then, he smiled.

With my expression still as cold as a block of ice, I said, "I didn't say you could sit." But then, I couldn't hold it in any longer. I busted out laughing and so did he. And in those moments when we were cracking up together, it felt like old times with X.

After awhile, we got our laughter under control and X said, "Listen Sasha, I just came here to clear the air. Since Friday, I feel like we've lived a lifetime, and all I know is that I don't want to lose my best friend."

I pushed myself up and moved around to the front of my desk. As I leaned up against it, the hemline to my already short skirt rose and I watched Xavier's eyes scan my legs. I waited for him to finally look into my eyes before I said, "I don't want to lose you either. It's just that when I couldn't convince you..."

He held up his hand and stopped me. "You don't have to convince me. Now, I'm not saying that I understand, or agree, but I know you well enough to know that you'll always listen to God. Eventually. And my prayer is that you will hear and listen to Him soon."

In a way, this sounded like another slam from X, but I let it go. He had come here so that we could remain friends and I respected that.

"So, do you forgive me?" he asked.

I nodded.

"And we're still friends?"

I nodded again, this time, a little harder.

He grinned. "That's what I want." He stood and pulled me into his arms.

I hugged him back, loving the familiarity of his embrace. When I finally pulled away from him, I smiled, but his forehead was etched with lines.

He stepped back, but he still held my hands as he said, "You have such a call on your life, Pink. I saw it the first time we got together, I saw it when we did the prayer line together, I saw how you led people to Christ."

I didn't know what Xavier was talking about. To me, he was the one who'd been called. He was the one who led our group, he was the one saving souls. I was just his helper.

Xavier kept on, "I want to see you walking in your gifts. I want to see you walking in the fullness of what God has for you."

A shiver shot up my spine and I trembled.

He frowned as he stepped away from me. "Are you okay?"

I nodded and crossed my arms. "I just got a little chill." Glancing up at the ceiling, I added, "Maybe it was the air conditioning." That was my explanation, though I felt as if the chill had come from the inside of me. It felt like there was a message inside Xavier's words, but I wasn't sure what it meant. Wasn't I already walking in the fullness that God had for me? Hadn't I been obedient since I was sixteen?

Even though I was glad that Xavier had stopped by, I felt even better when he said, "Well, I'm not going to hold you up any longer. I have a client in an hour, but maybe we can get together for dinner this evening?"

There were so many reasons why I wanted to do that, and so many reasons why I couldn't. It would've been nice to forget all that had gone down this weekend and just hang out, sharing a plate of sushi at The Thai House. Or splitting the pineapple upside down cheesecake from the Cheesecake Factory.

But I couldn't because hanging with Xavier like that wasn't my life anymore. I couldn't get sidetracked by the good times we'd had in the past. I had to stay focused. And my focus tonight would take me to my parent's house for the first part of my plan.

Xavier wasn't part of this plan. He couldn't go with me into my future.

"Maybe some other time, X," I said, trying to let him down gently. "I'm sort of busy here and I know it's going to be a long, long day. It'll be too late for dinner by the time I get off and by then, I'll just want to go home and chill."

Xavier knew me well. And I knew him, too. That's why I could tell that he didn't believe me.

He just nodded and said, "That's cool. Another time. So you're coming to Bible Study tomorrow night?"

Of course I was going to be there. *That* was part of my plan. But I couldn't tell him because I didn't want him arriving at the church, waiting for me, messing up what I had to do. So, I said, "I'm not sure. I want to, but this is going to be a crazy week at work. If I can make it, though, I'll be there."

He gave me another nod and then, he pulled my hand to his lips and gently kissed my palm. For the second time in just a few minutes, shivers swept through me.

"Have a wonderful day," he whispered in that voice that could have won my heart if I didn't already belong to Malik. Then, he walked out of my office without another word.

Even after he closed the door behind him, I stood there, still staring at the space that he had just occupied. That man right there had to be the sweetest guy I'd ever known. In another lifetime, it could have been the two of us.

I sighed. I was going to have to do something about Xavier because if I wasn't careful, he could become a distraction. Whether he was yelling at me or kissing me or talking to me, he took my focus away. Although I didn't want to do it, I was going to have to stay away from Xavier.

I'd figure out something, but I would have to do that later. Right now, I did have to get work done. Because unlike what I told Xavier, I didn't have a long day at the office. There was something I had to do right after work. Something I had to get done tonight.

Chapter 6

I pressed the code on the entry gate, then drove up the circular driveway of my parents' estate. It was just a little after seven and my plan was to get in, get what I needed, and then, get out.

Slipping out of my car, I walked across the cobblestone walkway, then, pressed in the second code that opened the front door. I pushed the twelve-foot tall door open and then, stepped inside.

"Hello."

My parents weren't home. Of course, I knew that. They were only into five days of their two-week vacation, but I wasn't sure if Mrs. Johnson, my parents' housekeeper/cook was home. When I heard nothing, I called out one more time, just to be sure. But all I heard was the echo of my own voice that reverberated against the oak walls of the entryway.

I closed the door behind me, then leaned against it as I looked up at the winding staircase. All I could do was smile as I remembered the times when I would slide down that wrought-iron railing. My brothers had taught me how to do it and boy, did they get in trouble when my mother came home one day and saw us sliding down, one after the other.

I chuckled. So much for me getting in and getting out. It was hard to walk into this house and not linger in the wonderful memories. It felt like so long ago when I'd called this place home, though it had only been four years since I'd left for college. I did come home the day after graduation, but a week later, I was in my downtown DC condo...a surprise gift from my parents. I was thrilled that my mother and father understood my need to be independent and out on my own. But I really did miss this house in the Northwest section of DC, in an area that many called the Gold Coast, but I just called it home.

Though, this was far more than an ordinary home. This was an estate, an eight thousand square foot Victorian style home that was worth millions now, but I know my grandfather had purchased it for a steal back in the sixties.

Growing up, though, I didn't know how privileged I was. I thought everyone lived in a huge house filled with love and a staff that met our every need. I was spoiled, there was no doubt about it. But I wasn't a brat. None of us were. My parents had raised children who had good minds and good manners.

And they exposed me to everything they could: I was a Girl Scout, a member of Jack and Jill, and a debutante in the Delta Sigma Theta cotillion.

My parents had raised me right and I would always be grateful for their love, their inspiration and guidance. Now, though, it was time for me to take care of myself. And so even though I wanted to walk through the house, and even sit in front of the grand piano in the living room, I didn't want to take any more time.

So, I rushed past the staircase to the room that was right off the patio—my father's study. I stepped inside, then locked the door behind me. That was just a safety precaution, in case Mrs. Johnson suddenly showed up.

It wasn't going to take me long to find what I needed. My father was neat, organized, and a creature of habit. Rushing to his oversized desk, I pulled open the drawer on the left, and there they were—a bunch of keys. If my father wasn't so organized, I may have been in trouble. But the keys to Grace Tabernacle were on a keychain that was still being sold in the church bookstore. I dropped the keys into my purse, closed the drawer, made sure that nothing else was out of place, then walked to the door. I pressed my ear to the door, and when I was sure that all was quiet, I stepped into the hallway. This time, I didn't linger. Sometimes it was nice to tarry in my childhood home. But not tonight.

Minutes later, I was in my car, driving away. And feeling very excited.

I had the plan all in my head. Tomorrow, Bible Study. Before I'd left for college, Malik always showed up to church an hour before Bible Study. I prayed that was still his practice. After that, I just had two questions—was the church alarm the same? And would Malik be alone?

Those were important questions because first, if the alarm wasn't the same, I wouldn't be able to get into the church before Malik. But I was hoping and praying that the code that my father had given to me years ago when he'd asked me to leave some important papers on Pastor Malik's desk was still the same code. It was a hard code to forget; it was the church's zip code. I remembered thinking at the time that that was the dumbest alarm code ever. Couldn't any street-smart burglar figure it out?

That's what I thought at the time, but it seemed that I had more confidence in burglars than they deserved because the church had never been broken into. I just hoped that the code had never been changed.

Then, there was my next question...would Malik be alone? That was as critical as the alarm because if Sister Stroman was with him, then my plan was shot. I would just have to pray, pray that demon away. I had to pray that God would clear the way for me, with the alarm and with that woman.

Chapter 7

The moment my digital clock's numbers flipped to 9:00, I picked up the phone.

"Good morning; Sasha Jansen's office; how may I help you?"

"Amber, this is Sasha."

"Hey, girl," she said and I rolled my eyes.

If I didn't have so much on my mind, I would've corrected her...again. When was she going to get that I was her boss? But, I couldn't think about that right now. There was so much I had to do between now and six o'clock tonight.

"What's up?" Amber asked.

"I'm not feeling well," I said.

"Really? You sound fine."

"Well, it's a stomach flu," I snapped. "It doesn't affect my voice."

"Oh."

She said that like she knew I was lying, but I didn't care. This was the first day that I was missing since I'd started working and I wasn't going to make this a habit. "Can you tell Bob that I won't be in today?"

"Okay." Then, she lowered her voice. "So, what's really going on? You getting together with that fine Xavier?"

"Girl. Bye!" I hung up the phone and wondered once again if it had been such a good idea to have a friend working with me.

But, there would be plenty of time to think about that and maybe even handle it. Right now, though, there were far more important things on my schedule.

I lingered in the bed a little bit longer, but within fifteen minutes, I was in the shower, and then, dressed and on my way to the full day of pampering. I'd actually called the manager of my favorite spa that just happened to be in my favorite hotel—the Four Seasons. I'd called last night and the manager had set it all up for me.

Of course, I was right on time for my 10:00 appointment and Michelle, the manager whisked me into the private area. First up was Joan, my manicurist, for a French tip manicure and pedicure. Next was my esthetician, Myra, who relaxed me with my herbal facial mask, and finally, Morgan, my stylist took over, adding highlights to my cinnamon-colored tresses. Then, she blow-dried my hair so that it hung straight, past my shoulders. By the time I walked out of that door five hours later, I felt like a diamond and looked like a million.

It was getting close to four when I arrived back at my condo. That gave me close to two hours to get ready. I'd chosen my black maxi sleeveless dress. Though it covered all of me, it showed just about everything since I'd had the designer dress altered to highlight my shape. Even still, it wasn't my sexiest outfit. But, it was sexy enough. I was going to church, after all. And really, it was sexier than anyone would know since I wasn't going to wear a stitch of underwear. That was going to be my secret. A secret that I just might have to share, depending on how Plan B played out.

The second hand of the clock on my bedside table ticked as I dressed slowly and carefully. Perfection could never be rushed. But right on time, I was in my car and ready for the twenty-minute drive to the church. Every part of the plan, every step of the way had been worked out in my mind. The greatest challenge that I would face would be me. I had no doubt that Malik would be mine after tonight. I just had to remember to be patient. Of course, he would resist at first. But that would all be for show. Once he had his lips on my lips and his hands all on me, it would be a wrap. He'd be mine.

As long as I remembered that, it would be cool. I had to take this slow and easy. I was the seductress and he would be seduced.

My car was the only car on the lot when I rolled into my father's space. This was exactly what I expected since it was only six and Bible Study didn't begin 'til seven-thirty. But just as I turned off the ignition, I frowned. Usually, I was so methodical in my planning, that I forgot nothing. Clearly though, it must've been my excitement that hadn't allowed me to think this all the way through. Parking here, in my father's space, right next to Malik's, would alert him when he arrived. He'd know that I was waiting for him inside.

I revved up the engine, backed out, and swung my car around the corner, finally stopping in the space behind the church that was reserved for receiving shipments. Malik wouldn't see me back here. The only problem—now, I had to walk on the pavement. I could end up with scratches on my red bottoms. But the prize was Malik, so I was willing to even sacrifice my shoes.

Sliding out of the car, my heart was pumping as I walked around to the front. It was a little bit excitement: I couldn't wait to be with Malik. And, it was a little bit anxiety: I wasn't crazy about acting like one of those street-smart burglars, breaking into the church. But there were times in life when you had to do whatever you could to get what you really wanted.

When I got to the front door, my hands shook just a little as I put my father's key in the lock. Then, my stomach lurched when the door clicked open. First step: accomplished. But then, I faced the blinking light and the soft beeps of the alarm. If it wasn't disarmed within a minute, the alarm would blare and the police would be here before I could get out of the parking lot. I took a deep breath, punched in the zip code, then squeezed my eyes shut.

And then...nothing. The alarm was off.

I reset it, though, so that Malik wouldn't know that I was here, though I left the motion detection off. My hope was that Malik wouldn't notice that little red light on the alarm. And if he did, he would just think that the last person hadn't set the alarm correctly.

The silence of the church felt strange as I walked through the hall that led to Malik's office. His door was closed, and I wondered for a moment if this was something else that I hadn't thought through. Was his personal office locked? But thank God, it wasn't and I stepped inside. Malik may not have been here, but I felt as if he met me right at the door. Not in the flesh, but in every other way. I could feel his presence in this room where he spent so much time. And, I could definitely smell him. The fragrance of his woodsy cologne was left behind.

In the half hour that I had, I wanted to study Malik and really get to know him. Using only the early evening light that shone through the windows, I took my time moving through his office, touching every part of him. My fingers trailed against the countless Bibles and commentaries and other books on his shelves. I studied his two degrees from Harvard University that hung on the wall, and then, I turned my attention to his desk. I admired the antique desk clock and the platinum pen and pencil set with his name engraved in each.

Then, I settled into the leather of his executive chair and I wondered if he had one like this at home. If he didn't, I would get him a chair like this—once we were married.

Smiling, I leaned back, but then, just as quickly, I frowned and sat up straight. I let an extra moment pass, just to make sure that I saw exactly what I thought. In two seconds, I had that picture of Malik and his ugly wife face down, flat on the desk. Then, I wiggled back once again in the chair.

I only stayed there for a few moments, before I stood and continued my journey. This time, I stopped in front of the closet that was partially open. I could see a couple of the robes inside and I reached for the burgundy one with the gold collar. Slipping it off the hanger, I slid into the robe and sighed. Of course, it hung off of me, several sizes too big, but I didn't care. I brought the collar up to my nose and inhaled. Closing my eyes, I shook my head slightly. The thought that went through my mind, was of course, a corny one. But it was so true; this was the way I felt at this moment. All I could think was: Be still my heart. I so needed this man.

The soft beeps of the alarm startled me. I stood still, but for only a moment. He was here. It was time.

Moving quickly, I returned the robe to the hanger, then rushed back to the desk. I wanted to be sitting there so when he walked into his office, he would see me first. In my head, I went through my plan again. Malik would walk in, he would see me, he wouldn't be able to resist, we would fall into each other's arms, and finally, I'd be his and he'd be mine.

His footsteps echoed through the hall. Coming closer and closer. My heart beat to the pace of his movement. We were in sync already.

And then, the door opened. And there was my king.

Malik flipped on the light, then stood there. He looked shocked, but he looked amazing. And even though he was feet away from me, the slight scent of him made its way to my nose.

"Pink?" he asked, as if he couldn't believe his eyes.

"Yes." I left off the rest of the words. What I really wanted to say was, 'Yes, my love.' But I kept thinking about patience. There was no need to rush this. I had to let him get used to the idea that I was here. I stood, so that he could see every inch of me.

His eyes took another one of those slow strolls down my body and I saw that glimmer in his eyes. The same glimmer that was there when he looked at me on Sunday. Then, he shook his head slightly, as if he really thought he could shake away his desire for me away. "Sister Pink, what's going on?" he asked as he placed his briefcase by the door.

It wasn't that I expected him to run over to me, but I was surprised that he stayed in place and didn't come any closer.

"I wanted to speak with you. Alone this time," I added, acknowledging that my prayer had been answered. Sister Stroman was nowhere in sight.

His eyes did that up and down thing again, but this time, he didn't even bother to meet my eyes when he finished. He paused right at my cleavage. I stood straighter so that he'd have an eyeful.

"You shouldn't be here," he said, sounding like his mouth was full of gravel. "How did you get in?"

To me, that was a dumb question, and I never answered dumb questions, no matter who was doing the asking. So instead of speaking, I just moved toward Malik until I stood right in front of him.

I had to crank my neck all the way back because without my signature stilettos, I was five, maybe six inches shorter than he was. I liked that. My father was that much taller than my mother.

I lifted my hand slowly and when Malik didn't move, I gently pressed my palm against the side of his face.

"I think you already know this, Malik," I whispered, "but, I've been in love with you since I was sixteen. Since you placed that ring on my finger." And then, I added, "And this has nothing to do with an infatuation. I'm a grown woman and I know what I feel."

He stood there, looking so deeply into my eyes, it felt like he was staring straight into my soul. My heart began to pump as if it was making its way out of my chest. This was it. I knew what was going to come next—he was going to accept this, he was going to lean over and seal our fate with a kiss.

When he bent toward me, I closed my eyes and parted my lips to receive him. But then, he grabbed my hand, and my eyes snapped open. Though his touch was gentle, his words were not.

"We're not going to do this, Sister Pink," he said almost in a growl, before he let go of me and strolled to his desk.

I had to blink a couple of times. There was so much wrong with this picture. Turning around, I watched as he settled into the chair where I'd just sat.

"What you're feeling is not love," Malik said with a sigh that felt so heavy. "You were young, and you still are."

"I'm not young anymore, Malik," I said, placing my right hand on my hip. "I'm old enough to know."

He blew out a couple of extra breaths. "Well then, you have to know that this is never going to work. I would never be able to reciprocate any feelings. I'm a married man, I'm your pastor, I'm...."

"You're making excuses," I said, stepping toward him. "Because none of that matters. Not if God really wants us to be together."

He chuckled a little, making a sound that I didn't like. "How could God possibly want that, Sister Pink?" he asked. Again, he shook his head and the glimmer that I saw in his eyes before had flipped. Now, I saw just a bit of pity. "Sister

Pink, you don't love me and God didn't tell you we were going to be together."

Sister Pink! Sister Pink! Sister Pink! Ugh! He sounded as steadfast as he did when he came by my condo. And I thought that he'd just said those things because he was there with his wife. Maybe it wasn't her. Maybe he really believed the things that he was saying.

No! The devil was a lie. Satan was just trying to get in my head. I knew the voice of God as sure as I knew my own name.

Malik's reaction just meant that I had to make a bold move. Something to show him, something to convince him.

I was right in front of him when the idea came to me. And, I did one of the things that I did best. I brought tears to my eyes and dropped my head into my hands. I sobbed and just like I knew Malik would do, he jumped up.

"Sister Pink..."

That was all he had a chance to say. I grabbed him in between his legs.

"Ah," he moaned, not sounding at all like he was hurt. I squeezed the part that made him a man. "Ahhhhhhhh." His moan was louder and longer this time.

He was as hard as a rock and I wondered just how long it had been since he'd been touched this way. He squirmed trying to release my hold on him, though I didn't think he was trying all that hard. But I held onto him like my life depended on it. In a way, it did.

It was going to take more than just me holding him like this to show him that I was a woman. I had to make this man see and feel all that he would have once he surrendered and did what God wanted.

With my right hand, I squeezed him as hard as I could. With my left, I slipped the strap off my shoulder revealing my left breast. Really, I wanted to let my dress drop all the way so that Malik could see and appreciate all of me. But, I couldn't release my grip. It seemed, though, like what I'd revealed was enough. Malik's eyes bulged, though his face was still twisted in his sweet pain. I could've just blown on him and he would've toppled over. Instead, I gave him a little shove, and he fell back into his chair.

It was the lessons that Xavier had given me that let me move so speedily, so accurately. It hardly took seconds for me to unbuckle, unzip and have his bare manhood in my hand. And just a second after that, he was in my mouth.

His hands were on my shoulders, pushing me away. But I didn't move. Or should I say that nothing on me moved, except for my mouth. Up and down. Down and up. And then, his hands that had been offering resistance, now were on the side of my head moving with me. Up and down. Down and up.

All kinds of mutters were coming out of his mouth, almost like he was speaking in tongues. I was sure that he was trying to say my name, but I couldn't even enjoy this moment, this first time that we were united. This was a "job" to me, literally. I had to concentrate on making him feel good, making him see that all of this talk, all of this Sister Pink this and Sister Pink that, all of this resistance was pure foolishness.

I sucked in my cheeks, a move that was porn-star worthy. And it didn't take long before Malik's groans filled the entire room. He was moaning like he didn't care who heard him.

Then, he shivered. For what seemed like an hour. But really, it was just seconds. And it was over.

When I looked up, he was still sitting back. His eyes closed, his breathing quick and shallow.

I slipped the strap of my dress back onto my shoulder, then grabbed a tissue from Malik's desk. Moving quickly, I picked up my purse and stepped toward the door. It wasn't until my hand was on the doorknob when he called out, "Sister Pink," sounding like he had just run a marathon.

But, I didn't even turn around. Whether he wanted to say thank you, or ask when we would get together again, or tell me some more of that Sister Pink nonsense, I wasn't going to stay around to listen. He'd have to come and find me.

And, after what I'd just done to him, I knew that he would.

Stepping into the hallway, my first thought was that I couldn't believe how perfect God's timing was. Right there, right in front of Malik's office, I came face to face with Sister Stroman. Actually, God's timing could have been just a bit better. Because if she had been here just a few minutes sooner...

I brushed my hair back off of my shoulder. Then, with the tissue that I still held in my hands, I dapped at the corner of my lips. I was sure that my lipstick was quite smudged—which was a very good thing at this moment. "Good evening, Sister Stroman," I said, like she was one of my best friends.

Her mouth was too wide open for her to get a word out. In her eyes, I could see all of her thoughts and all of her questions.

Wearing victory, I walked down the hall and out of the church. There was no need for me to stay for Bible study. I'd already received my message and I'd just delivered a message. No, I'd delivered two—to Malik and his soon-to-be ex wife.

Chapter 8

My mind was on Malik through the entire drive home. I remembered the way he tasted, the way he felt, and I especially remembered the way he moaned. He had moaned like he had never felt anything as good as my mouth.

Inside my condo, I went about my business. I took off my dress, wishing once again, that I'd been able to do this in Malik's office. Then, I stepped into the shower. Under the cool shower spray (I never took hot showers. The hot water dried and aged your skin) I closed my eyes and lingered in that feeling of victory. I was really thrilled that Malik had been so pleased.

After ten minutes, I dried myself off, moistened my skin, then wrapped myself in my silk robe. When I sat at my vanity and began brushing my hair with my natural bristle brush, I stared at my reflection and admired the woman who looked back at me.

I'd had so many lonely days and even more lonely nights as I kept myself for Malik and now, tears sprung to my eyes. Not because I was sad in any kind of way. It was just the opposite. This was finally the time, this was the place, he was the man.

I really didn't want to sit here and cry because really, I needed to be celebrating. I rose from the vanity and strolled, into the kitchen. A nice glass of Moscato was exactly what was called for. After filling up a flute, I strolled into the living room and grabbed a magazine. It was too early (just about nine) and I was too worked up (with all kinds of thoughts in my head) to go to bed. So I flipped through the magazine, checking out the competition. This was something I often did for work, though skimming through magazines and checking out the ads didn't feel much like work to me.

I didn't look up again, until my cell phone rang. And when I glanced at the screen I was surprised that an hour had passed. But, I wasn't surprised by who was calling. It was a little before ten now, and Bible study lasted two hours. So this call was right on time.

"Hello, Pastor," I said.

There was silence for a couple of seconds. Not that I could blame Malik. The sound of my voice had probably brought back all kinds of memories. He was probably hard right now, just hearing me. It was a wonder that he was even able to carry on with Bible study. Or maybe he didn't. Maybe Xavier had covered for him, and all he'd done was sit in his office and imagine being with me.

Finally, he said, "Sister Pink."

Really? After the intimacy we just shared, he was still calling me Sister? He was really going to have to drop that. Unless we were role-playing or something.

"Malik, if you don't mind, I'd prefer that you call me Sasha. Just Sasha."

"Sasha." He said my name so softly. Then, I heard him clear his throat. "Sasha," he began, "I have to apologize. For what happened."

I frowned. "You don't have anything to be sorry for. You didn't do anything." I wanted to add that I'd done all the work, but I didn't think that would help.

He said, "Yes, I do have something to be sorry for, and yes, I did do something. Because I should've stopped you."

"Trust me," I said. "There was nothing that you could've done to stop me."

"Well, something has happened that made you think, made you believe, that what happened, was right. It was so wrong, Sister Pink," he said, slipping right back into that Sister thing again.

I flopped back onto the sofa. *Oh, my God!* I was gonna have to go through this with him again? Was he still going to resist what God was trying to put together?

He said, "I wanted to share a scripture with you that came to mind after you left."

Well, that was one good thing—his mind stayed on me exactly the way I expected. Not that I thought he wouldn't be thinking about me.

Malik said, "The Bible teaches us that the flesh is weak, but it is the Spirit who makes us strong."

"Yes, I know that scripture very well, Malik," I said, trying not to sound annoyed. But I really was. How many more mountains was I going to have to climb with him? Why was he putting up all this resistance? Didn't he know that he would never win in a battle with God?

"Our flesh was weak," Malik continued to preach to me. "But I know that with prayer, we can build up our Spirit man to resist temptation. We need to get on our knees and pray, Sister Pink."

Oh, lawd!

"We need to pray and not only ask God for forgiveness, but ask Him to lead us not into temptation and to deliver us from this evil."

I rolled my eyes and said nothing.

Malik didn't seem to notice. He was on a roll. He said, "Because Sister Pink, it was wrong. I'm a married man."

That was when I had to jump in. Yes, he was married, but to the wrong woman. "I know you're married, Malik. But at the same time, I know that tonight was meant to be."

"Sister Pink, I really need you to hear me. What happened tonight will never happen again. I won't be a part of committing adultery. I'm a holy man, an upright man."

Yeah, yeah, yeah! Blah, blah, blah!

"We need to pray together, Sister Pink."

If this man didn't stop this!

"Will you pray with me?"

I wanted to tell him no, that all of my prayers had been answered. But I had to show him what kind of wife I was going to be. So in the most submissive voice I could muster, I said, "Yes, Malik, I will pray with you."

"Okay. Are you sitting down or are you on your knees?"

I almost laughed out loud. Did this man really want me on my knees? Didn't he remember what had happened the last time I got on my knees?

"Do you want me to kneel down?" I whispered.

There was a moment of silence, a cough, and then, Malik said, "No, no, no. You can sit up...if you want to."

That's what I thought, I said to myself.

Malik started praying, "Father God..." and I strolled back into the kitchen.

As he prayed about forgiveness and the evils of temptation, I recorked my bottle of wine, put it back into the refrigerator, and then returned to the living room. I returned the magazine to the rack, fluffed out the cushions on the sofa, then turned out the lights. By the time Malik said, "Amen," I was tucked away in my bed.

"Amen," I said, just a moment after he closed out the prayer.

"Thank you, Sister Pink."

"You're welcome," I said sweetly, though I was rolling my eyes all over the place.

"Well, goodnight. And may the Lord forgive us both."

With a sigh, I clicked off my phone and stared at the screen for a moment. The devil was really trying to make this hard, but Satan had picked the wrong one. I was not going to be defeated. I was not going to be denied.

Slipping down beneath my satin duvet, I clicked off my bedside light. Tomorrow was another day. Tomorrow was another plan. Plan C would be in full effect.

Chapter 9

For the last two nights, I'd slept like a baby.

And both mornings, I woke with a song on my heart. This morning, just like yesterday, I was smiling when I rolled out of bed and onto my knees. As always, I kept my morning prayer short. God knew what I was going to pray before I did.

"Thank you, God, for all the blessings, especially the one you've given me with Malik. Amen."

As I moved toward my bathroom, there was an extra pep in my step. Maybe it was because I'd made it past Plan B and now, I was headed to Plan C. I wasn't happy that I still had to manipulate this situation, but that was going to change soon. Malik and I would just have to go all the way. We'd have to consummate our relationship and then, it would be game, set, match!

There was just a single thought going through my mind as I showered quickly. How was I going to get Malik alone again? I didn't quite have that answer, but I knew it would come to me. Like yesterday, I was out of the door in less than an hour compared to the almost two hours that it always took me to get ready. I was movin' and groovin'. I was happy.

I wondered if I'd always be like this once Malik and I were together. Would his love always keep me upbeat like this?

The sun was shining and even the traffic was light as I drove to the office. It wasn't even eight-thirty when I pulled up into the parking garage. I couldn't remember a time when I'd been to work this early. I'd even beat Amber to the office.

But nine o'clock sharp, Amber bounced into my office. "Hey, girl."

"Amber!" I snapped, as I looked up from the spreadsheets on my desk.

"Oh, sorry," Amber said in a tone which made me believe she wasn't sorry at all. "Anyway," she said, keeping her voice stiff and professional this time, "I wanted to remind you that you have a ten-thirty meeting."

"Thanks," I said, looking back down at the Profit and Loss statements I was studying.

"And also, your mom is on hold. Should I put her through?"

Why didn't Amber start with that? My mother was on the phone? Was she calling me from Fiji?

"Definitely!" I said. "Put my mother through."

Seconds later, my phone buzzed. "Hi, Mother! Are you in Fiji?"

"No, sweetheart, we're home."

I frowned. "Home?" They'd just been gone a week. "Why did you come back early?"

"It was such a long flight," my mother said, ignoring my question. "And we are just exhausted."

"Okay," I said slowly, wondering what was up.

"But Fiji is a beautiful place and I hope you get to go there sometime."

Just when I was about to ask my mother what was up, she told me.

She said, "I'm calling because your father wants you to come to dinner tonight."

My stomach flipped, doing somersault after somersault as I wondered why in the world would my parents want to have dinner tonight? If they were so exhausted, why couldn't this wait for tomorrow night?

In my head, I went over my movements through my father's office. I was very careful when I was there on Monday when I got the keys and last night when I returned them. My parents were so meticulous, I made sure that everything was in place.

"So, dinner at seven," my mother said. It was a demand, not an invitation. That's how it always was with my parents.

"Yes," I said as a formality more than anything else. "I'll be there at seven."

"And not a minute later," she said.

That was her good-bye. A moment after that, I heard the click. Before I had returned the phone to its holder, I was shaking. And not with good anticipation. I was nervous. But then, I began to think that I was making too much out of this. Maybe it was just that my parents couldn't wait to see me. Maybe they'd bought me some wonderful gifts. Or maybe one of my brothers had come to town and they were going to surprise me at this dinner.

There was really no way for me to guess. So what I needed to do was just get my attention back to work. I needed to get these reports done.

It wasn't as hard for me to concentrate as I thought it would be. In fact, having something else to concentrate on helped to keep my mind off of the dinner.

But when I turned the reports in, my mind was free to wander again. It was just noon and I wished that it was already seven so that I could already know why my father had demanded my presence?

My plan had been to start another project and keep working through lunch, but then, I thought that maybe getting out would distract me. I definitely wasn't hungry, but maybe a little retail therapy would help.

Right as I picked up my purse, Amber buzzed me. "Hey, girl," she said.

I shook my head, not even bothering to say anything this time.

"That fine-ass Xavier is on the phone. You want me to put him through?"

"Yes," I said a little more enthusiastically than I expected. I'd just vowed the other day to stay away from X. But seeing him right now was exactly what I needed. He would be able to take me away from the anxiety I was feeling. So, I picked up the phone. "Hey, X, how you doing?"

"Great! I'm downtown just finishing up with a client and I'm not too far from you. How about lunch?"

"I'm not really hungry, but you up to going for a little stroll?"

"That sounds good to me. Come on down," he said, mimicking the host of *The Price is Right*.

The smile that he put on my face was genuine and the pep that I'd felt in my step this morning was back. I slapped on my sunglasses right as I walked out of the building and then, I almost took them off so that I could get a better look at Xavier. Amber was right. His ass sure was fine. He stood there in a pinstripe navy suit with a crisp white shirt and a pink tie. I grinned.

He was handsome, and so professional, but that tie, really set it off.

"You look great," I said as we hugged.

When he stepped back, he looked me up and down. "But I don't look anywhere as good as you."

"Thank you, sir," I kidded him.

As we began walking up 12th Street, Xavier took off his jacket and swung it over his shoulder. "I have a meeting later," he explained. "Don't want to get too sweaty."

I chuckled. "I thought you were too cool to sweat."

He laughed, then said, "I missed you at Bible Study on Tuesday."

Instantly, my pre-Bible-study meeting flashed through my mind: Malik, his office, the taste of him.

"Yeah," I said. "Remember, I told you that this was going to be a crazy-busy week at work?" I kept my eyes looking forward, not wanting Xavier to look at me that closely. He could always read me and if he was able to see into my mind right now, I don't know what he would think.

"But, you're not busy today."

"What?"

"Today," he said. "You're not too busy to get out for lunch."

I knew he'd said that because he didn't believe my excuse for missing Bible Study. All I said was, "I just needed a little break." Then, I added, "I was glad that you called."

Through my peripheral vision, I could see that Xavier kept his eyes straight ahead, too. I guess he didn't want to look at me either. I guess he was afraid of what he might see.

He didn't look at me, but he held out his hand and right away I took it. I reveled in the comfort of what was so familiar. It felt so good. We walked that way, together, saying nothing for a couple of blocks. Then, I told him, "I've been summoned home."

Now, he looked at me and when he frowned, I smiled.

"Nothing bad," I said, hoping my words were true. "My parents are back from their trip. My mom called this morning and said that I have to be there at seven o'clock sharp!" I was trying to make light of the demand that I'd been given to come home. "I've been called to the big house."

Xavier laughed. "You always make it sound like you're an inmate and your daddy is the warden. Girl, I've seen that mansion where you grew up."

Xavier had been to my home only once. The day after we arrived back in D.C. and my parents had not been welcoming at all. Thank God, X hadn't taken that out on me.

He said, "You grew up in a wonderful place. You've been blessed."

"Yeah, I have been," I said.

"Yup. So many of us never grew up with both a dad and mom who loved us."

I tilted my head as I looked up at him. "I know that, but thanks for that. Sometimes I really do need that reminder."

We went back to our silent stroll, turning right on H Street.

"Hey," Xavier said, stopping and then looking up. "Let's stop here and I'll grab a quick sandwich."

We stepped into the small sandwich shop that was fill with the noon-time crowd. Xavier ordered a turkey breast on wheat, while I ordered chicken noodle soup.

"As hot as it is woman, that's what you want?"

I nodded, and tried to laugh it off. But the truth was, I didn't really want to eat a thing. I was just hoping that the soup would settle my grumbling stomach.

As we sat, we chatted. He told me about the wrongful death case that had been all over the news.

"Do you think that cop will get away with it?" I asked about the policeman who'd shot a sixteen-year-old boy who attended Suitland High School.

"Not if we can help it. I'm the junior attorney, but we're all putting in long hours. What's going on with you?" Then, he clarified, "What's going on with you at work?"

"Nothing as exciting and meaningful as what you're doing, but I hope to be the first junior editor promoted."

"You always want to be first," he kidded me.

"Isn't that one of the things you like about me?" I asked.

Without missing a beat, he said, "That's one of the things that I love about you."

We looked at each other for only a moment, and then both of us looked down and away. As if that word love should've never been uttered between us.

Like I always said, at another time, in another place, Xavier would've been the one.

Still, I was having such a good time with him, until he asked, "So, did you work all of that stuff out with Pastor?"

At the mention of Malik, the memories flipped through my mind like flash cards. Again, I lowered my eyes. There was no way I wanted Xavier to see into the mirrors of my soul.

But I couldn't look down forever. And when I raised my head, Xavier was shaking his. "You know," he began, "I once thought that you had the prettiest eyes I'd ever seen. But now..."

I narrowed my eyes and glared at him. "What does that mean?"

"You're so lost," he said, without missing a beat. "And for the life of me, I can't figure out how it happened."

My stomach growled again, but this time it wasn't from anxiety. What gave him the right to judge me like this?

"How did you get to this place?" Xavier asked me, softly. "How did this happen?"

"I've already told you but I guess you need to hear it again."

"No, I don't. I just don't understand why you're so confused."

I folded my arms across my chest.

He continued, "I'm not trying to be mean, and after we made up on Monday, I'd promised myself that I wouldn't get into this with you again. But when you didn't show up to Bible Study..."

"What's the big deal about that?"

He shook his head. "I just knew that something wasn't right. I almost called you when I left church, but I fought it. And, I fought it yesterday and this morning. And even when

I called you to go to lunch, I promised myself that I wasn't going to say a word. I was just going to get together, check on you, and I was going to leave it at that.

"But seeing you now, and like this...I can feel it, Pink," he said with such pity in his voice. "Something terrible is going to come from this."

Then, he leaned across and when he placed his hand over mine, I snatched it away. But that didn't seem to upset him.

"Pray, baby."

"I pray every day," I said. "You know that. I pray every morning as soon as I wake up."

But it was as if I hadn't said a word. "God wants you back," Xavier told me. "He will forgive you, and you can start again."

Oh, my God! For a moment, I wondered what Xavier knew. Had Malik told him? No! He would never do that. This was just conjecture on X's part.

But, I couldn't sit there and let him think that he was right. "What are you talking about? I haven't done anything that I need to be forgiven for."

"We all need forgiveness, baby," Xavier said, standing up. "We all need prayer."

I stood with him because now, I was so ready to go. We walked out of the restaurant, but it was totally different from the way we'd come in. Now, we didn't talk, we didn't touch. Both of us were locked in our own thoughts.

I knew Xavier was thinking about what he'd told me. He thought he knew what was going on. But he didn't know anything. Not unless God had told him. And if X had heard from God, he would know that what I was doing was right, what I was doing was the truth.

In front of my building, Xavier stopped and finally spoke. "I only talk to you this way because I care, not because I want to get caught up in your business."

"And I appreciate that you care about me. But you have to know that if I'm doing what God told me to do, if I'm doing what God placed on my heart, then He will take care of me."

He moved his head from side to side and in his eyes I could see that he felt so sorry for me. Right then, I knew this was the end with Xavier.

He said, "You know, today, for the first time, I really think you believe what you've told me."

Was he kidding me? Did he think that I'd made all of this up before?

He stood still, as if he was waiting for me to say more and when I didn't, he pressed his lips against my cheek with a kiss that told me I was right. Whatever we had between us was over. Then, he turned and walked away.

I was glad that he was gone. There really wasn't room for him in my life.

So, if that's how I really felt, then why did I feel so empty and alone as I watched him walk away?

Chapter 10

I was beginning to have my doubts. For the first time, I began to doubt what God said to me. Maybe doubt wasn't the right word. Maybe the right word was wonder. Because after being with Xavier, that's what I began doing. I began to wonder if I'd been wrong?

I was determined not to let confusion take over me, but when I got back to my office, I did feel the need to pray. So, sitting behind my desk, I closed my eyes and clasped my hands together.

"Dear, God," I began. And then nothing. I didn't know what else to say. After a few moments, some more words came to me. "Am I doing the right thing?"

Then, I just sat there because I knew that the Bible said we needed to be still if we really wanted to hear from God. So I sat at that desk, doing nothing but keeping my hands clasped and waiting. I knew God would give me something, at least some kind of feeling. But even after an hour I didn't feel any different. All I heard were Xavier's words echoing in my head. Now, I was mixed up—all because of X.

What I needed was my mother. I had always been able to speak to her about everything, though I had never shared *this* secret with her. But maybe now was the time. She knew my relationship with God. She was the one who'd taught me how to pray. She'd believe me and she'd give me advice on exactly what I needed to do to get Malik. Even though my father wore the pants in our family and he was clearly the head of his house, there was no doubt that my mother played her role, too. The reality of it was, my mother had my father eating out of the palm of her hand.

That's what I needed, Mother's advice. As I rushed into the bathroom to freshen my makeup (because I could never show up to my parents' home without looking like I'd stepped off the pages of a high-fashion magazine) I prayed that I would have a little time alone with her tonight.

But once I got into the car, my thoughts shifted back to the summons and the reason why they wanted me home tonight. Xavier kidded about me feeling like a prisoner, but sometimes that's how I felt. Not in a bad way. My daddy loved me. But, he was like a warden. His word was gospel. It was the beginning and the end. And if you ever did anything to make my father upset...I shook my head.

"This is your daddy, Sasha," I said to myself as I glanced in the rearview mirror. "You're going to be fine. You don't have a thing to be worried about."

That was my mantra as I maneuvered through the winding curves of Rock Creek Park. But my own words did little to calm me. I truly felt like trouble was waiting for me in the hills of the Gold Coast.

Chapter 11

The moment I put my key into the lock and twisted it, I heard the grandfather clock that was in the grand foyer of my parents' home chime seven times.

Stepping inside, I paused for a moment. "Hello," I said, though I said it so low, someone had to be standing right next to me to hear my voice

My heels clicked against the marble floor as I moved toward the living room, but then, Mrs. Johnson came from around the corner behind the staircase.

"Hello, Sasha," she said, always so formal. Before I could even say hello to her, she said, "Your father would like you to meet him in his study."

That was a bad freaking sign. His study? My parents always met me at the door; always so overjoyed to see me. And the few times they didn't do that, they were waiting for me in the living room. But his study? That meant that he knew that I'd broken into the church.

I was already trying to think of lies as I made my way to daddy's study. I almost felt like I was taking that last walk down the hall to Death Row. The door was partly open, but I still knocked. Not because I was being polite, but because I was trying to buy just a little more time.

When I stepped in, I put on the biggest smile I could fake. But I was the only one smiling. My mother sat in one of the chairs in front of my father's desk with her legs crossed at her ankles and her hands clasped in her lap. Even though her face was stiff and stern, my mother looked amazing, like a golden Queen. The sun in Fiji had tanned her caramel complexion to a toasted shade of nutmeg. It really stood out against the burnt orange sleeveless dress that she wore. But it was her shoes that really caught my attention. She was rocking a bad pair of snake skinned Louboutins.

If it weren't for the look on her face, if I weren't so scared, I would've asked her where did she get those shoes? But instead, I just said, "Hi, Mother. Hi, Daddy," and then kissed my mother on her cheek.

"Hello, Dear," my mother said, then patted the arm of the chair next to her.

I took the seat, doing as I was told. Turning my glance and my attention to my father, I said, "Daddy, you look great." I smiled, hoping that compliment would soften his stern expression as he stood behind his desk holding a glass of brandy. Then, I added, "You do, too, Mother."

With just a little nod to me, my father slowly walked around his desk until he stood directly in front of me. My heart was pounding, and then, my father leaned over and softly kissed my cheek.

That calmed me for a moment. Until my father glanced at my mother. When she nodded, I frowned. It was like my father was asking my mother's permission to talk to me. Something was up because this certainly wasn't his style.

Leaning back against his desk, Daddy said, "Sasha, your mother received a disturbing phone call Tuesday evening. It was so upsetting that we packed our bags and caught the first flight we could get home."

My thoughts were whirling. A phone call? From whom? Tuesday was the night I'd been with Malik. Had he made that call?

I didn't know what to say.

But then, my mother explained, "Sister Stroman called and she's made some serious accusations against you."

I breathed a little, feeling half-relieved. At least it wasn't Malik. But was Sister Stroman any better? What had Malik told his wife? Surely he wouldn't have told her what I'd done?

My parents both stared at me as if they were waiting for my explanation, but I wasn't going to incriminate myself. I wasn't going to say a word until I knew what they knew.

I was sick about this. My plan was to have this all worked out by the time my parents got back. The news would've been a shocker to my family, but once they saw me and Malik together, and once I explained God's plan, my parents would have understood.

But here I was in the middle of the plan and so I didn't know what to say.

I guess my mother got tired of waiting for me because then she added, "Sister Stroman said that you've been flirting with Pastor and that you've made her and Pastor and everyone around uncomfortable."

Flirting? Okay, that was good. I mean, not good, but better than the truth. Still, I just sat there, silent and stiff.

"I'm sure most of what she's said was not true," my mother said as she waved her hand in the air like Sister Stroman's words were a lie. "Because I just cannot imagine you behaving the way she said. But she did call us for advice, so we need to know what's going on?"

When I still didn't say anything, my father added, "We need some answers, sweetheart. The things that Sister Stroman said..." He shook his head before he continued. "She actually insinuated that you've made very inappropriate advances toward Pastor Stroman."

"Yes," my mother picked up, "she made it sound as if you were practically throwing yourself at Pastor." My mother held her hand against her chest as if she just couldn't fathom such a thing.

I looked from my mother to my father and at that moment, all I wanted to do was cry. My parents had so much faith in me, they always had. And all my life, I'd try to give them every reason to have that faith. From my youngest days, I always wanted to be the best daughter, the perfect daughter, with perfect grades and perfect plans. No matter what my mother wanted me to do, I did it—piano lessons, dance classes, charm school. And then, there was church. I was in every church play, sang in the choir, and even helped out in the Children's Church.

I'd done it all, and I'd done it well. So, why did I feel so small, and like a child right now?

I guess it was because for the first time, I had to face the fact that I was bringing shame on my parents. Sitting here, right now with what I'd done, maybe I wasn't the great daughter. And even though I hadn't technically had sex with Malik—yet—I could be considered an adulteress, something I knew my parents would never be able to imagine.

"So," my mother said, "is any of this true?"

There was a part of me that just wanted to lie, that just wanted to keep up the facade of the good daughter. It would've been so much easier. But I didn't want to. I didn't want to keep this secret anymore. I needed to explain it all to my parents. And maybe they would do what no one else had done. Maybe they would believe me.

So, I whispered, "Yes."

"Yes?" my parents said together.

"Yes!" I said, almost shouting it this time. "Yes!"

The way my mother clutched her chest, I thought she was going to have a heart attack. The way my father just stood there with his mouth open, I thought he was going to faint.

"Oh, my God! What are you thinking?" my mother said.

I jumped up. "It's true," I cried. "I love Malik. I have always loved him."

"You can't love him!" my mother shouted. "He's married and you weren't raised that way."

My father added, "And he's your pastor. He's older."

"None of that matters to me. None of that matters to God."

"Sasha," my mother said. "Listen to yourself. It doesn't make sense."

Ugh! Here was another person calling me crazy. That was when I snapped. "I don't care what you say," I sneered at my mother. "I love him and I'm going to be with him. So everybody better just get used to it."

My mother moved so fast, I didn't see it coming. She jumped up and in the same move whipped her hand across my face, stinging my cheek. Stunned, I just stared at her, too hurt to move, too hurt to cry.

"As long as you live," my mother said in a voice that was low and deep, "don't you ever forget who I am. I am your mother and you are never to speak to me or your father like this ever again! Do you understand me?"

I just sat there, holding my cheek, hoping that all my teeth were still in place.

"Do you understand me?" my mother repeated.

I was afraid that she was going to take another swing at me, so this time, I spoke up. "Yes, Mother," I said being extra careful to be extra polite.

Then, my mother stood up straight, and continued as if she hadn't just about knocked the hell out of me. "Now as I was saying, Pastor Stroman is married. He loves his wife, he doesn't want you and we are not going to let you make a fool of yourself. All of this craziness is going to stop right now, do you understand me?"

Slowly, I nodded. What else was I supposed to do? My mother being against me was like the final blow.

My mother kept talking as if I hadn't heard her, as if I didn't feel small enough, "You have been raised to be respectable, honest, and trustworthy. Throwing yourself at a married man is not on that list, do you understand?"

I nodded. The tears finally came, filling up my eyes, though I blinked to keep them back.

"There are plenty of young men in the church who would love to go out with you." I turned my head slightly to face my father. I'd practically forgotten that he was here. After my mother slapped me, my whole world had become blurry.

"Yes," my mother said. "In fact, Sara Wallington's son is about to get his doctorate. Maybe I'll give her a call."

Did my mother think it had really come to this? That I needed her to set me up on a date? Did she think that what had happened with me and Malik was like that? A game that I could play today and stop tomorrow?

All I wanted to do was get out of there. I didn't need to say anything else, and I certainly didn't want to hear another word.

"Well," I said, slipping the strap of my purse back onto my shoulder. "I'm going to go now."

"Go?" my mother said as if she were surprised. "But you haven't had dinner."

Was she kidding? They had just berated me, she had just slapped me and called me every kind of fool. And I was supposed to just sit down to dinner as if this hadn't happened?

"Sasha, we want you to stay." My father came closer to me and I swear that if he touched me, those tears I was holding back were going to fall. "Stay," he whispered. "Have dinner with us. We want to tell you about our trip."

See, the thing about my parents was that they didn't realize that I was grown. Yes, they could tell me what they wanted, but they couldn't tell me what to do. They couldn't make me stay for dinner, and they couldn't make me stay away from Malik, no matter what they thought. But since my cheek was still stinging, I kept my thoughts to myself. All I said was, "I'm sorry, Daddy, but I have to go." I gave him a quick peck on his cheek. And then, I did something that I had never done before. I walked out of the room without giving my mother a hug nor a good-bye.

I moved quickly, hoping that I would be out of the house before the shock of all of that wore off on my parents. But just as I put my hand on the front door knob, I heard my mother call, "Sasha."

My mother had been right. I was raised to be respectable and that meant that I didn't disrespect my mother. So when she called my name, I stopped. By the time I turned around, she was right beside me.

With a deep breath, she took both of my hands into her own. "I'm not sure how all of this came about," she said softly, "but I'm telling you, baby, you have got to stop whatever you were doing. You've got to give this up." I looked down, but she lifted my chin with the tips of her fingers. "You're a smart, beautiful girl and you've always made us so proud. Don't turn around now. Don't give in to the ways of the world. Stand strong in your faith and wait for God to send you your mate. Because your man is out there. The man has been chosen for you."

I froze. Those were the same words that God had spoken to me. So my mother *did* know. But if she did, why had she just acted that way? Was it all just a show for my father?

But then, she said, "So, you'll forget all about this foolishness with Pastor Stroman?"

I nodded because my mother was right about one thing—I was smart. And I wasn't about to say or do anything so that she would slap me again. So, I hugged her and said, "Yes, Mother."

When she leaned back, she was smiling. "So, you'll stay and have dinner."

"No." I turned around and walked out of the house. Without looking back, I knew my mother was still in the doorway. Even when I got in the car, I didn't look back. I kept my eyes straight on the road until I pulled out of the long driveway. Only then, did I look in the rearview mirror.

"I don't care what they say," I told myself. As I aimed my car toward home, I was more determined than ever.

Chapter 12

To the rest of the world, it may have seemed as if I'd given up, but I was just buying my time. The most successful people in this world had patience, I was about to start acting like Job.

I behaved as normally as I could. When I'd left my parents' house on Thursday, I called them when I got home the way I always did. And, I even chatted with my mother when she apologized again for slapping me.

"I was just so surprised when you admitted it," she'd said. "I hope you never give me a reason to do that ever again."

"I won't, Mother," I said, meaning that. There was never going to be a time, ever again, when I was going to put myself in the position where my parents were so angry that one of them wanted to hit me.

On Friday, I spent a normal day in the office and on Saturday, I returned to the scene of the crime. My mother once again summoned me to dinner (though this time, it felt like more of an invitation.) And this time, both of my parents met me at the door with hugs and kisses, nothing like the way I'd been greeted on Thursday.

It would have been a wonderful evening with my parents, talking and laughing and looking at all of their photos from Fiji. I say *would have* been because although there was a smile on my face, my heart was very heavy. I was being kept away from the love of my life, when all I wanted to do was move forward and be with him.

I hadn't yet figured out my next step, hadn't yet determined what my Plan C was going to be. One thing was for sure, it was going to have to be a military-type covert operation because now that my parents had been drawn in, the stakes were higher.

I still couldn't believe that Sister Stroman had actually called my parents. While they were in Fiji! As God as my witness, I was going to make that chick pay. Before, all I was going to do was take away her husband. But now, not only was I going to take Malik, but I was going to figure out something that would make her so sorry that she'd had the audacity to mess with me. Before, I was going to be gracious and let her even continue coming to Grace Tabernacle. But now, she would be lucky if I let her live in the DMV area.

But as much as I wanted to plot my revenge, I couldn't waste my time thinking about Sister Stroman. At least not right now. All of my energy had to go into Malik...and how I was going to handle church this morning. All eyes were going to be on me, of course, though Malik's eyes were the only ones I cared about. But it seemed that my parents were being extra cautious about me. So cautious that I guess they weren't going to let me out of their sight, which is why my mother had just called me, I suppose.

"We'll pick you up, Pink," she said lightly, though I could hear that wasn't a suggestion, it was another one of her commands.

"Pick me up?" At first, I had no idea what my mother was talking about, but then it hit me. She wanted me to ride with them to church. Really? I hadn't done that since they'd given me my own car when I was sixteen.

"Yes," my mother said as if her question was the most normal question in the world. "This way you'll save money on gas..."

Save money? Really? Saving money was the last thing that my mother cared about, so was I really suppose to believe this? Was I not suppose to recognize this for what it was—a way to keep me close and away from Malik?

There was no way I was going to debate this with them. Never again. I wouldn't say another word about my man...not until we were together and then, there would be nothing they could say.

"Okay, Mother, that sounds great," I said as if I really meant that.

For now, I'd go along with this program. Let my parents—and Sister Stroman think that they'd won.

So, I told my mother that I would be ready, and then, I dressed, taking particular care in what I wore. I'd have to dress conservative enough for church—and my mother. But, I needed to be provocative enough so that Malik would notice, and remember. Maybe I wouldn't have to come up with a plan. Maybe Malik would take one look at me today, would realize that our souls were meant to be tied together, and would be as tired of waiting as I was. Maybe he would stand at the pulpit and confess his love for me and declare God's plan for us so that everyone would know and we could move on.

My parents were already waiting when I went down to the lobby of my building, as if they wanted to make sure that I didn't slip away and go to church on my own. As I sat in the back of their Bentley, I chatted as if my heart wasn't pounding. As if I wasn't nervous about seeing Malik for the first time since we'd been so intimate.

In the church parking lot, my stomach jumped a little when I saw Malik's car already parked in his space. My parents didn't say a word as we all slipped out of the car, then I walked in between them as we made our way toward the church. As my father opened the doors for me and my mother, he said, "I'm going to the office to see Pastor Stroman." He glanced at me as he said that, like he was waiting for me to say something.

I stared blankly, not saying a word.

"Go ahead," my mother said as she turned her cheek to the side for my father to kiss her. "Pink and I will go in and take our seats."

My father kissed me and then, my mother took my hand. Yes, literally, she took my hand like I was a child, like she wanted to make sure that I didn't run away, and she led me into the church where the praise team was already standing up and rocking the sanctuary.

My mother led me to the left side, the second row, right behind Sister Stroman who was already in her seat. As I slipped into my seat, I glared at Malik's wife as she turned around and squeezed my mother in a hug. With my eyes, I shot daggers at the back of her head, but when she faced me, I gave her a smile.

And she gave the same fake smile back to me.

I went back to shooting those daggers when she turned around and I kept on, even when my father joined us. But once, Malik strutted out onto the altar, my eyes were only on him.

Just like always, he took my breath away when I looked at him. But I was really affected this time because all I could think about was Tuesday. When I'd held him and tasted him and pleased him. I saw that scene over and over in my head. I remembered his moans and his groans and the way I'd made him scream out in pleasure. I remembered the way he'd looked at me when I revealed my nakedness (as much as I could) to him.

All I wanted was to do that again.

Even when Xavier stood to greet the guests, my mind was still on Malik. But then, Xavier went over the church announcements.

"And, finally church, this coming Saturday, will be resuming the Single's Ministry."

I sat up straight as "Amens" rang through the sanctuary.

"As Pastor Stroman announced last week, Sister Sasha," he paused and glanced at me, "and I will be heading that up and we look forward to the first meeting. This Saturday at three o'clock."

"You didn't tell me that, Pink," my mother said as she patted my hand with approval.

I wondered when she thought I should've told her about that. Was it before or after she'd slapped me?

"I think that is such a great idea," she whispered.

All of a sudden it was a great idea that I was doing something with Xavier? My mother must have forgotten that she didn't like X. But, I guess he was far better than Malik.

I spent less than two seconds on that thought, though. My mind was spinning. To this point, I didn't have any idea how I was going to get back together with Malik, and now, I had it. I couldn't wait.

This Saturday at three o'clock.

Chapter 13

It was if God Himself had spoken.

That's all I could think as I sat in the back seat of my parents' Bentley still mesmerized by the entire church service. If I hadn't heard the announcements myself, if I hadn't listened to the sermon, I wouldn't have believed it.

I really wanted to dash home and just let everything that had happened seep into my spirit. But I couldn't because Mother had insisted on having brunch, and since I wasn't driving, I had to do what my parents wanted. Although it was really all right with me. I was hungry, famished, and nearly bursting with joy. My love had heard from God and he poured out God's word as though it was meant for he and I alone.

"Let's go to the Howard Theatre," my father said as we pulled out of the church parking lot.

"That would be delightful," my mother said. "I just love their gospel brunch."

As my parents chatted about how much they both loved all the renovations that had taken place at the theatre, I tuned them out, though if my dad had glanced in the rearview mirror to look at me, he would have never noticed. There was a huge smile on my face. It was the same smile that had been there since Xavier had made the announcement about the Single's Ministry and had given me this idea. And then, my smile had just continued straight through Malik's sermon. His message was even better than the sign that I'd been given from Xavier.

"Pink, honey we're here."

I was so into my thoughts I hadn't realized that we had made it to the theatre. Daddy had already stepped out and was handing his keys to the valet, along with giving the young man a long list of instructions about how to park his precious Bentley. I waited along with my mother until another valet attendant opened our doors.

Once we stepped into the beautifully refurbished Howard Theatre, we were greeted by the Maitre'd and whisked away to my father's private booth. My father had been a huge contributor in the reconstruction of the theatre and the Mayor had shown his appreciation by telling my parents they would always have a private booth whenever they came to the theatre.

As we followed behind the host, my mother stopped. "Excuse me," she said to Daddy and me. "I see a few of my Sorors."

While my mother took a turn to the left, my dad and I slipped into our booth and I immediately picked up the menu. We were silent for a couple of moments until my dad said, "Pink, what are you going to have today? I think I'm in the mood for a few pancakes and bacon."

I chuckled. I could never ever eat like that, at least not without feeling bad about it. "I'm not sure yet," I said, keeping my voice light, as if I were really happy. I was, but there was no way I'd let my parents know the reasons why. I needed them to believe that their little talk and that big slap had affected me. Once they were disarmed, then, I could get back to Plan C.

"I think I'm going to have the salmon salad," I said to my father. "You should have something lean like that, too. All of those pancakes and bacon isn't good for you."

My father chuckled and I did, too. But I kept wishing that my mother would get to the table so that she could monopolize the conversation like she always did and I could get back to thinking about Malik's sermon that just wouldn't leave my head.

And as soon as my mother came back, she took over the small talk and I was able to turn my attention to all the thoughts in my head.

As my mother chatted about an upcoming fashion show, I half-closed my eyes and went over the entire church service. First, Xavier had given me all that I needed for Plan C. And then, Malik had stood in the pulpit with his eyes directly on mine and he had given me the go ahead. He'd told me exactly what he wanted me to do.

"Church, open up your Bibles to Genesis the nineteenth chapter, verse twelve," Malik had said. "My sermon for today, is: When it's time to go, go!"

I pushed lettuce from side to side on my plate, as I thought back to how Malik had given me the signal that he was ready to move forward with me. I was beginning to fall in love with the spiritual connection that was happening between us. Malik had said, "Church, when the three men came to Lot and told him to take his wife and two daughters and flee the city of Sodom, it was God's way of letting him know that he could either be obedient or he could die along with the rest of the people who were evil doers. How many of you guys are ready to die?"

He paused as the parishioners looked around at each other.

He continued, "How many of you are ready to live the way God intended for you to live?"

Hands were raised all over the sanctuary, but it wasn't until Malik got to the nitty-gritty of the sermon, when I knew for sure that I was doing the right thing. He had stepped down out of the pulpit, then, as he talked strolled over and stood in front of his wife.

"Church, when God says go, you better go. When God says, don't look back, you better go and not look back. Lot's wife loved the city so much, she wanted to look at it one more time before they fled and when she did, she was turned into a pillar of salt.

"Well, I'm not looking back. I'm going on, moving forward and I'm not going to turn around. I'm not going to let anyone tell me what God has for me, because God has already shown me my expected end."

With every word my love spoke, chills went up and down my arms. I even shivered a time or two and a few tears of joy tumbled down my face. He had just told the congregation that he was going to leave his wife.

I shouted, "Hallelujah," and I didn't even care when my mother gave me the side eye.

I was so sure and so happy that Malik was now on board. I wasn't naive, though. I knew that he might still need a little bit of a push from me. Not convincing; he just needed to know that I was willing to do anything to get him. So, I was really glad that I'd been shown how to move forward with Plan C. Plan C would surely seal the deal.

⇜⇜⇜

For the next week, I stayed as far away from Grace Tabernacle as I possibly could, which wasn't easy because of my parents. I had to stay in touch so they wouldn't suspect a thing.

So, on Monday, I phoned my mother:

"I won't be able to make Bible Study nor Wednesday night prayer," I told her.

"Oh, sweetheart. I hate it when you miss church. Why not?"

"I have to go out of town," I'd lied. "To New York. They put me in charge of interviewing a few students for our internship program."

"That's wonderful! You're already moving up at the magazine."

I could hear the pride in my mother's voice, and it made me feel a little bad that I was lying like this. But it was all for the best. It was the only way that I could fulfill God's plan.

And some of my guilt was assuaged when my mother told me to shop as much as I wanted in New York and she would pay my American Express bill.

"My treat," my mother had said.

There was no way I wasn't going to take her up on that offer. Of course, I wasn't going to be in New York, but I did need something new for Plan C. So, during my lunch hour at work on Tuesday, I visited the LaPerla website and ordered the pure white Symphony Rock underwire demi bra and matching bikini. That was the extent of my shopping.

I don't think a week had ever moved so slowly for me. As it got closer to Saturday, my nerves were on fire, but I remained as cool as I always had. On Thursday, I had told Amber to take the day off so that she wouldn't ask any questions when I left early on Friday. Then on Friday, I headed over to the Four Seasons spa to have my hair touched up. Morgan nearly jumped from her skin when I suggested that she give a sexy up-do style.

On Saturday morning, I was almost trembling with excitement. So, I decided to take a nice cool soak to calm myself. While I rested beneath the sudsy water, I prayed once again. "God even if they don't believe, I believe. I trust You and I'm willing to do whatever I need to do, to do you will."

When I stepped out of my Jacuzzi tub, my thoughts turned to Xavier. I had half-expected him to call me about the Single's meeting today. We had never talked about it and it wasn't like Xavier to do anything unprepared. But I guess he really was done with me. And he was only going to be around me when he had to. That made me sad, in a way, but it was the right move. Plus, I wouldn't be heading up the Single's ministry much longer.

For the rest of the morning, I lounged around, played Adele, and snacked on a fruit salad. At two-thirty, I imagined that Malik and Xavier were already at the church, expecting me to show up at any moment. At three, I was sure that the church was filling up with expectant singles, all waiting to hear a Word that would help them find their mate.

At three-ten, my cell phone rang. I took a deep breath before I glanced down at the picture. It was Xavier's picture that filled my screen.

I pressed 'Ignore,' then went into the kitchen and popped open another bottle of Moscato.

After a few sips, my nerves calmed. After a few minutes, my cell phone rang again. This time, it was Malik's picture on the screen, and I pumped my fist in the air. My first thought was to let the call go to voicemail. But, I couldn't take the chance of him not calling back. So after the fourth ring, I turned on the water works and answered.

"Hello." I sniffed two, three and four times.

"Sister Pink? Where are you? Are you okay?"

"No, Pastor, I'm not. I'm so confused right now." And then, I bawled.

"Sister Pink, what's wrong? I was calling about the Single's meeting, but clearly, God led me to call you for another purpose."

You got that right.

I just kept crying.

"Sister Pink. What is it? Please, tell me."

The distress in his voice showed me how much he cared.

"Pastor, I'm so ashamed of what I've done, so ashamed of what I did to you. I just can't face anyone, I don't belong on Holy ground."

At that moment, to use one of Amber's terms, I turnt' up. I mean, I boo-hooed, I sniffled, I coughed as though I was choking.

"Sister Pink, please stop crying. What happened was a mistake, but God gives us second chances to get it right. Let me pray with you, please?"

I was so hoping he would ask me that. I had even prayed to God that Malik would say this and this was just more signs that God had ordained my mission.

I sniffled as though I was trying to stop crying. "I don't think I can pray Pastor."

I practically heard his heart beating through the phone. He waited a moment, but I wasn't going to say another word. I kept on pretending that I was trying to gather myself—to no avail, of course.

"Would it help if I came over? Together we can get a prayer through. Would it be all right if I came to your home to pray with you?"

Booyah!

"Yes, Pastor," I cried. "I really need to go to God and you're the only one who can help me."

Chapter 14

The time had come, but I had to admit, I was nervous. But still, I looked up and clasped my hands together. *Thank you, Lord.*

After tonight, there would be no more worries, or plotting, or planning. The days and nights when I would yearn for him would be no more. On this evening I would tie my soul to his, finally.

I couldn't help but think back to the night that had started me out on this journey. When I'd stood before Malik and heard the voice of God. *The man of God for you has been chosen.*

Not a day has gone by when I didn't repeat those same words. Everyone had called me foolish, but I'd hung on to what I'd heard from God. And, I'd hung on to Malik's words, too.

"True love waits," he'd told me as he slipped that ring onto my finger. Well, I'd waited long enough.

The sound of the intercom snapped me back and when the concierge announced that, "Pastor Stroman is here to see you," I said, "Send him up."

The man of God for you has been chosen.

As I took a final glance in the mirror, I wrapped my short-pink baby-doll robe over my new La Perla goodies and stepped out of my slippers. I leaned forward to check out my make-up. It was messy; my mascara was smeared as if I'd been crying all day. Perfect!

For an added effect, I smudged my lipstick and added a little extra blush because I needed that flushed look. I held my eyes open wide until tears sprang fourth and started to roll down my cheeks.

All that was left to do was open my Bible. I turned to the scripture that confirmed my mission: Genesis nineteen and I sat it on the settee. But I only had a few moments before the doorbell rang.

I took a deep breath and added one more prayer. "Please God. Please let him be alone."

I was sure that he would be since he was coming straight from the church and not from home. I was holding my breath when I opened the door and didn't exhale until I saw that my prayer had been answered.

"Sister Pink," he said gently and then took my hand.

I pushed a sob up from my throat and he stepped inside, closed the door behind him, and then, he held me. I laid my head on his chest and sobbed like a baby. Malik rubbed my back and whispered soothing words about God caring, God loving me, God understanding.

"All you have to do is ask for forgiveness," Malik said, "and God will forgive it all. From one end of the ocean to the other, He has tossed your sins aside."

"But I don't think He hears me. How can He after what I've done."

"Yes He does. He hears, He knows, He cares and you have to believe that. Now, are you ready to pray?" Malik asked that question with so much sincerity in his voice it almost made me cry for real this time.

Once again, he took my hand and lowered his head. But, I didn't want to do this standing. So still holding onto him, I began to kneel and tugged him to follow along. He hesitated, but only for a moment and he knelt, too. His eyes moved from mine, to the settee where my open Bible rested.

When he looked back at me, I asked, "Malik, do you forgive me?"

His eyes moved from mine and I watched him swallow as he took in my shoulder, where my robe had somehow fallen from my shoulder. I knew what he saw—my very firm breast that was barely covered by the thin satin. He could just about see my nipple.

"Malik," I whispered, squeezing his hand just a little. "Do you remember what I did to you? Do you forgive me?"

He could hardly speak as he closed his eyes and inhaled. "Father, God," he began, as if he would really be able to pray now.

He continued though, and I slipped my hand away from his. He didn't open his eyes, as if he knew what was happening. As he kept talking to God, I slipped my rope completely off my body. But, I didn't stay silent.

"Yes, God, thank you, Jesus," I said behind Malik's words.

He prayed for a good two minutes straight, with his eyes shut so tightly, I wondered if he would ever be able to see again. But then, he said, "Amen," and he slowly lifted his head, then opened his eyes.

And I was right there waiting for him. Every single inch of me. His eyes took in my barely-covered breasts to the pink diamond that pierced my belly button, down to my French-tipped toes.

"Sister Pink." He moaned my name.

Before he could say another word, I wrapped my arms around his neck, and then, went limp, as if I'd fainted. Or maybe he thought I'd been slain in the Spirit. Whatever it was, Malik did exactly what I knew he would do. He lifted me into his arms and carried me toward my bedroom.

At first his steps were quick, but they began to falter as I softly kissed his neck. When he looked down at me, I nudged my face closer and closer to his mouth until we were lip to lip.

"Pink."

He'd dropped that Sister thing and I knew I had him at his weakest moment. By the time we made it to my bedroom, and he placed me on the bed, it was a done deal.

I laid there in my virgin white panties and bra, with my virgin body, plump in all the right places, glistening with pure almond oil and smelling fresh as a spring morning.

He stood frozen and just took it all in. It was as if his feet were planted and he couldn't move or blink, hear or speak.

I reached my arms up to him. "Please," I said. I knew that simple word (along with my body) would be enough.

Malik laid down beside me and this time, when I pressed my lips against his, I used my tongue, gliding it against his lips, then introducing my tongue to his.

The walls of Jericho came tumbling down.

Malik was so gentle as his hands roamed and searched and lingered in places on my body that had never been touched. His kisses were as sweet as I imagined they would be. And they were tender, until they turned rough and hungry. It didn't take Malik any time to strip me nude.

There was only one problem—he was still in his clothes.

I knew I had to move fast before Malik came to his senses. So, I turned him over and climbed on top, straddling him. I kissed him—his lips, his face, his neck. As I kissed, he caressed me—my arms, my butt, my thighs. When he finally cupped my breasts, we moaned together.

"Ahhhhhh..."

Even though I knew I had him then, I still couldn't get him out of his clothes fast enough. I tossed his monogrammed shirt onto the floor and took in the definition of his chest.

Oh, my goodness, this man was so fine. Malik was so fine; I couldn't wait to see the rest of him. So, while he touched and kissed, I unbuckled his belt and after a little tug-of-war, I released him.

With my hands firmly around his manhood, I began to ease my body down his, leaving behind a trail of my sweet young sap with a scent that even I found intoxicating. When I finally reach my destination, I felt Malik hands in my hair releasing the pins that was holding my up-do in place.

I covered him with my mouth as my hair tumbled over his thighs. "Ahhhh..." He moaned at first. And then, he found his voice. "Oh, Pink, that feels so good."

I worked him, but just enough to get him started. I didn't want him to finish in my mouth. I wanted him to finish inside me, with us mating, with our souls being tied together forever. So, I lifted my head and called his name, "Malik."

Without saying anything else, he understood what I wanted. I had broken all of his resolve and Malik took over. I felt like the student being taken to class by the master of love-making and with every, "Oooh," and "Ahhh," he touched, kissed, suckled and licked until we were both breathless, until there was only one thing left to do.

I laid on my back and he tried to enter me.

"Pink," he said, as he pushed through.

His eyes widened with just a little bit of surprise. It was as if he didn't know I was a virgin. But hadn't I told him that? Didn't I promise myself to him?

He asked, "Pink, are you…"

I didn't give him a chance to ask me such a foolish question. What did it matter anyway. I brought my lips to his and squeezed my eyes shut while he went all the way in.

"Oh," I moaned. "Malik. Yes. Yes." Tears flowed from my eyes and I couldn't stop myself from crying. Mostly because it hurt so bad, or maybe because it felt so good, but mainly because he was finally mine.

We rocked and rolled together and nearly an hour later, we both lay, completely sated. I was exhausted, but I felt like a new woman. No, I felt like his woman.

After many, many minutes of silence, Malik opened his eyes, rolled over and faced me. "Pink, you know what *we've* done here wasn't the right thing to do, don't you?"

His words were shocking to me. After what had just happened, after the beauty of what we just shared, these were his first words to me? I refused to even acknowledge his question.

I rolled over, turned my back to him, then scooted my butt closer to him so he would feel the warmth of what he had done to me.

"Sister Pink?"

Oh. My. Goodness. What was wrong with this man? How could he have taken me in every way possible a man could take a woman and still call me Sister Pink?

I wasn't his sister, I was his soul-mate. But I guess Malik didn't have the clarity I said.

"Sister Pink, we need to pray."

Why did we have to pray? My prayers had already been answered. I needed to straighten him out.

"Malik, please stop calling me Sister Pink. My name is Sasha and I would prefer you call me by my given name."

He took a moment before he said, "Okay, Sasha, but that doesn't change the fact that we need to pray. What we've done tonight is a sin. Please pray with me."

I decided not to fight him on the praying thing because I loved the Lord as much as he did. And since Malik was my given man, my chosen man, I had to be submissive to him, just as I would be as his wife.

And anyway, we had already sealed the deal. I needed to pray and thank God. So, although my body was sore with the sweetest hangover, I followed his lead.

At the side of the bed where we'd just committed this sin, we both got to our knees.

"Dear God, please forgive us. Forgive me for yielding to temptation. God I pray that Sister Pink will forgive me for not being strong enough to resist, for not leading her into the right direction. Amen"

The moment the last word slipped from his lips, Malik jumped to his feet and searched the floor for all of the clothes I'd stripped for him. I leaned back on the bed, keeping my naked body in his sight, and feeling glorious and victorious. I didn't care that he was rushing to leave. My body was reeling from the affects of his lovemaking, and I needed some time to myself. Plus, this was Saturday night and if I were going to be the best first lady ever, I had to allow him time to prepare for Sunday service.

Once Malik was dressed, I stood and walked over to where he was standing. Putting my arms around his waist, I once again laid my head on his chest. Although he wrapped his arms around me, his embrace wasn't as gentle as it had been when we laid together.. "Sister Pink, no one can know about this."

"About us?"

He stepped away from me, looked into my eyes, and that was the first moment when I knew for sure that he would be back.

But still, he said, "No one can know about us. I'm your pastor and a married man."

I knew it would take a little more time for him to divorce old lady Stroman but I wasn't about to let him keep throwing it up in my face. "I won't tell anyone because I know what you have to do."

"I'm glad you understand because this can't happen again."

I just stood there and wondered who he was trying to convince. I looked at him and then looked to my bed. "You see that, Malik?" I pointed to my blush colored sheets that were now stained crimson. "That's the evidence of sacrifice. I saved myself for you just as I promised I would."

Malik dropped his head for a moment and when he looked up, I knew he remembered those words I had spoken to him six years ago. He opened his mouth to speak, but then he changed his mind. He just pecked me on my forehead and walked out of my bedroom.

I followed him to the door and there, he gave me a little kiss again. "Please, Sister Pink, this has to be our secret."

With my head, I nodded, but in my mind, I was planning my wedding and practicing my new name.

Mrs. Malik Stroman. Mrs. Sasha Stroman. The Reverend and Mrs. Sasha Stroman.

"Okay," I said.

This time, Malik kissed me on the lips, opened the door and walked out.

I closed the door, leaned against it, then strutted back to my room. At any other time, I would've removed any stained or soiled sheets. But not tonight. I laid for a moment on the side where Malik had been, taking in the fragrance of his cologne. I closed my eyes and imagine I was still wrapped in his arms.

Then I heard knocking.

Oh, my goodness. Malik was back. There was something in his eyes that told me he wanted more, but I didn't expect him to return so soon. I grabbed my robe, jumped up, then made my way to the door.

I was already talking before I even opened the door. "I knew you would be back."

Then, I stood frozen.

"Hey Sasha," Xavier said as he stepped by me.

All kinds of thoughts were going through my head. How did Xavier get in?

I said, "What are you doing here?"

X paused in the middle of my living room and when he glanced back at me, I felt naked. I pulled my robe tight to my body, though I knew he could tell I didn't have on anything underneath.

His eyes scanned my body, but not in a lustful way. He glance was full of disgust. "I came over here to see if you were all right," he said. "You missed the Single's meeting."

"Sorry 'bout that."

His eyes narrowed. "As I was coming in, I saw Pastor Stroman leaving."

"You talked to Malik?" I asked. My mind immediately filled with questions. What had Malik told Xavier?

"No," Xavier said, shaking his head. "He didn't see me. And, I didn't even know for sure if he'd been here to see you." He paused, and he looked me up and down once again. "But, I guess I know now." Then, without a hint of what he was going to do, he rushed toward my bedroom.

I ran after him, even grabbing his arm, but he jerked away from my grasp. He didn't go all the way inside, though. He stopped at the doorway and stared at the disheveled bed.

"What have you done?"

I wasn't sure he was really talking to me since he didn't face me. His eyes were still on my bed.

"Xavier, please leave."

"You slept with him?"

He didn't really have to ask me that. He already knew. I didn't owe him any kind of explanation, but I was so tired of this back and forth between us.

"Yes, okay," I admitted, "he was here and we were together."

The way X lowered his head and covered his face with his hands made me think that he was going to cry. "What kind of pastor am I serving under?"

"This is not Malik's fault," I said, defending him. "This is God's plan."

He glanced up once again and looked at me as if he'd never known me. "So, is this what you wanted? To commit adultery? What is wrong with you?"

"You don't like me? You don't like what I've done? Then, just get out of here!"

His face was creased with anger and he stepped close to me. "So, how does it feel, Sasha? Do you feel more like a Christian? Do you feel closer to God? What's it like to sleep with a married man? What's it like to be his jump-off?"

"Get out!" Go! Now!" X turned to leave, but he didn't move toward the door. Instead he grabbed me. At first, I didn't know what he was going to do. Xavier wasn't violent, but anyone could snap at anytime.

But then, as his grasp on me tightened, he squeezed his eyes shut and prayed, "Dear God, Father help my friend, God. Please God help her. I know she believes she's being led by you God…"

I tried to wrestle out of his arms. I didn't need him praying for me. "Let me go!"

"God forgive her, Lord, please." X released me and nearly ran from my bedroom. By the time I got to the door, he had already walked out, leaving my door open and my heart aching.

I screamed after him, "You don't know anything. I don't care what you think."

But, really I did care, because X had been my friend. The dearest friend I ever had. And I loved him, I think. But, now he was hurt, and now he was gone.

For a moment, I was worried. Would he run back to the church and confront Malik? Would Xavier tell everyone? That could have been a problem. But then again, maybe it wasn't. Maybe X would tell the people who mattered in the church and it would speed up the process of Malik and I being together.

So, I calmed myself, laid down on my bed, and began to hum…*Victory is mine, victory is mine, victory today is mine. I told Satan get thee behind, victory today is mine.*

Chapter 15

"Will a man rob God?"

As I sat in between my parents I had total happiness on the inside. Every part of me still tingled; it was so hard to sit still and contain all of my joy. From the moment I had entered the sanctuary with my parents, I'd stood with the choir, clapping, and swaying, and praising God with everything within me because there was so much that I had to be thankful for.

There was only one thing wrong—the devil kept trying to play with me. Images of Xavier and the way he'd looked at me, then, held me, and prayed for me were all in my head. I had to work hard to block those pictures and X's words from my mind.

Even now, as Malik spoke from the altar, all I wanted to shout was, "Preach, baby! Preach!" But instead, I couldn't stop thinking about Xavier and the way he prayed for me and how he tried to preach to me. And now, I had a bigger question and bigger concern: where was Xavier?

I'd been shocked when Malik had walked into the sanctuary and Xavier wasn't with him. There wasn't a service, a Bible study, or a prayer meeting that X ever missed when he was in D.C.. But today, Malik had walked out alone.

When I didn't see X at first, I tried my best to glance around the sanctuary, casually, as if I weren't looking for anyone in particular. I'd had to stop when my mother gave me a side-eye glance. I wasn't trying to draw attention to myself with my parents. I'd driven my own car to church this morning, though my parents had timed our arrival so that we could walk in together. Even though more than a week had passed, since my mother had tried to slap my love for Malik right out of me, they were still being cautious. And, I was doing everything I could to act as if I were carefree, as if I had not a concern in the world. So, when I glanced around the church, I didn't want my mother to ask me who was I looking for? I didn't want my mother asking me why was I concerned about Xavier? I didn't want my mother asking me anything.

But in the short time that I'd had before I had to turn back around, I didn't see, Xavier. And, I kept asking myself where was he?

I shook my head, wanting to get rid of all thoughts about Xavier. My focus had to be on my love. Malik and I were one now, in every way and he alone deserved my full attention. So, I kept my eyes on him.

But unlike the last two weeks in church, he didn't look at me. I kept my smile wide and my eyes wide and bright. I wanted him to look at me and see just how happy he had made me. And, I wanted him to look at me and show me how happy I'd made him. But, each time he happened to look in my direction, he quickly diverted his eyes.

Still, I kept my eyes on him and tried not to look at that empty chair on the right side of the pulpit. Xavier's chair. And just like that, my thoughts went right back to him. Was he just running late? Or maybe he had car problems. I tried to think of every excuse because I wouldn't be able to handle it if Xavier had stayed away from church because of me. One of his favorite things to say was that nothing could ever separate any of us from the love of God. I just prayed that I hadn't become that one thing that could make Xavier go against what he believed.

"Will a man rob God?" Malik said again.

I frowned because though my mind kept wandering, I kept going back to Malik every time he said that. And this was at least the fourth time. Why was he saying that over and over again?

This sounded like a tithing message and I couldn't recall ever hearing Malik preach about tithing before. Tithing and bringing our offerings to the church was just something that everyone did at Grace Tabernacle. Our church did more than survive, we thrived because the members gave willing. We were one of the richest churches in our district.

"Church, turn your Bibles to Malachi three verse eight."

All around me, folks pulled out their iPads, booted up their Kindles, and opened the Bible apps on their smartphones. Only a few flipped through the pages of the Bible the old-fashioned way.

"Church, I will ask you again, will a man rob God? Yet ye have robbed me. But ye say wherein have we robbed thee? In tithes and offerings." He slammed his Bible shut as if that was the final word. Then, he said, "Church, we've been robbed."

As mumbles rumbled through the sanctuary, dread settled in the pit of my stomach. It was not only Malik's words that made me feel sick, it was his tone. Never in all the years that I'd heard him preach, had I heard such anger in his voice. His tone was sharp and cutting.

Suddenly, I felt myself perspiring. With just a little glance, my mother looked at me and took my hand. For just a second, I felt relieved, until I looked back at her. It was the way she smiled, in a wicked kind of way, that let me know she knew what Malik was going to say.

"You heard me right, Church," Malik shouted, but not in that 'Hallelujah, thank you, Jesus,' kind of way. His voice was on the edge of rage.

"You heard me right, Church, we've been robbed. I was hoping that I wouldn't have to tell you this, I was hoping that somehow the checkbook that the deacons couldn't find would just pop up. I prayed that God would allow this bitter cup to pass. But now, after speaking with the detectives this morning...." Malik paused to not only let his words settle, but he had to stop for a moment because the loud mumbles began again. The congregation finally settled down, but my stomach didn't.

Malik continued, "But now after speaking with the detectives I have to face the facts and the facts say that our own Minister Xavier has robbed our church!"

This time a roar rolled through the sanctuary. The sounds of shock and anger filled the space.

While many turned in their seats and spoke to the person sitting next to them, I couldn't move. I could barely think, I was so stunned.

Mother turned to me and whispered. "Your daddy never trusted that boy."

The way she kept her eyes on me, I knew she wanted me to say something and I wanted to, but even if I had words, I couldn't get them out. I was absolutely speechless.

There was no way that I could believe this. X would never steal anything. He was a true man of God. He loved the Lord and he loved Grace Tabernacle just as much. There had to be some mistake and Malik had to know that.

I watched as Malik just stood back, letting the members of Grace Tabernacle go on and on about 'that thief, Xavier.' And as I stared at him, I wondered why would Malik even bring this to the congregation? Shouldn't he have spent more time trying to get to the truth? Because the truth was, there was no way that Xavier could do or would ever do this. He deserved the benefit of the doubt since he'd been such a good and true servant of God.

But as the members of Grace Tabernacle settled down, so did I. I might not believe what Malik said about Xavier, but Malik was my man. This was probably my first lesson in being a good helpmate. So, I had to stand by Malik. If he believed that Xavier stole from the church, then, I would have to believe it, too.

The anger that I felt throughout the sanctuary troubled me, and I didn't miss the way a few people directed their stares toward me. All I wanted was for this service to end. I had to talk to Malik, find out what was going on, and maybe even say a few words on Xavier's behalf.

Malik was finally able to get the services back on track, and as he moved through the rest of the message and then the altar call, I sat there, almost trembling with anxiety. I was ready to jump up when I thought Malik was going to begin the benediction, but instead of ending the service, he said, "I'd like my wife to join me, today." He held out his hand gesturing toward Sister Stroman and I wondered why did he want that old birdbrain up there with him?

But after he gave the benediction, he stood, side-by-side with his wife and greeted the parishioners.

At first, all I could do was stare at my man and his wife. But then, I calmed down. Malik was just doing what he had to do for now. As I slowly made my way toward the aisle, I pulled out my phone and texted Malik: *I need to see you, I'll be waiting!!!!!*

Just a few seconds later, I turned around and watched Malik as he un-clipped his phone and read my message. Even from where I was standing, I could see the ends of his lips curl into a small smile.

I was satisfied. I had no doubt that in just a few hours, I would be with my love. All I had to do now was wait.

⤝⤝⤝

It had taken a minute, but I was finally able to break free from my parents. Over and over, my mother had said, "Are you sure you don't want to join us for brunch?"

It wasn't until I told my mother that I had plans with Amber that she finally stopped asking. I hated that I had to keep lying to my parents, but this was the way it had to be until Malik and I were finally together. I had no doubt that once Malik spoke to my parents, they would be thrilled. They would understand that I wasn't infatuated, I hadn't made it all up in my head. Once it was a done deal, it would be better for everyone.

Rushing home, I picked up my phone more than a few times, checking to see if Malik had texted me back. Not that I really expected him to. I knew he would just come over. But still I checked because I also hoped that I'd hear something from Xavier.

Once home, I changed into a pair of pink silk boy shorts and a matching bra, then paced back and forth in my bedroom as I held my cell in my hand. I paced until I was tired, and finally laid across my bed. It wasn't that I was tired, at least not physically. But, I was exhausted emotionally. So much had happened in the last two days. I'd finally gotten together with my love, but I'd lost my best friend. As much as I wanted to, I couldn't get Xavier out of my mind.

I jumped up, startled when the intercom rang in my living room. Had I fallen asleep that quickly? I dashed to the intercom and when the concierge announced, "Pastor Stroman is here to see you," I breathed.

"Please send him up," I said.

I was as anxious as I'd been yesterday, but this time, it was for a different reason. Yes, I wanted to have Malik again. I wanted to feel his kisses and his hands all over me. But first, I needed Malik to tell me that somehow he had made a mistake, that he had found the checkbook, that X was innocent.

He had barely knocked before I swung the door open. But I didn't even get a chance to ask him a single question as he pulled me to him. With his hand behind my hand, he filled me with a feverish kiss and before I could catch my breath, he lifted me from my feet and carried me in his arms.

"Malik," I tried to call his name between his smothering kisses. I wanted to slow him down, talk to him first. But, I don't even know how it happened. I was sure not more than thirty seconds passed before I was undressed and underneath Malik.

I felt like he was devouring me, like a tiger that hadn't been fed in months. This time, his lovemaking wasn't as tender. This time, it was urgent. He kissed me and pounded me as if he wasn't sure that he would ever have enough. He hardly stopped...until he did, an hour and a half later.

I'd been ravished, but I felt great. There were so many sides to Malik and I loved it. I rolled over to talk to him, to tell him that, but when I heard that snore pass through his lips, I decided to let him be. Malik falling asleep thrilled me. If he felt comfortable to actually sleep in my bed, then we were closer to being a couple than even I thought.

I wasn't sleepy, though, so I leapt from the bed, cleaned myself up in the bathroom, then strolled into the kitchen to get something to eat. While I loved how Malik had just loved me, I still needed to talk to him. I still wanted him to answer my questions.

About ten minutes later, I sauntered back into the bed with a cut grapefruit on my plate. I had planned to eat and flip through magazines until Malik woke up, but I was surprised to find that he was already awake. He was sitting on the side of the bed, wearing nothing but his briefs.

There were so many things I wanted to do to him and so many things I wanted him to do to me at that moment. But, I had to keep my focus on what had been bothering me since I entered church this morning.

"Malik," I began as I sat the grapefruit on my nightstand, "what happened with X? Is it true what you said this morning?"

He brought his hand down across his face as if he was wiping something away. Then, without looking at me, he said, "I don't want to talk about it."

"But..."

"Don't but me!" he exclaimed as he jumped up. Now, he looked at me with squinted eyes. "The checkbook is gone and Minister Xavier was the last person in my office."

Malik had always been so gentle when he spoke to me, but now, his tone was filled with the same anger that I'd heard this morning.

"Stealing is not even in Xavier's nature," I said, determined to not back down, determined to know. "He wouldn't do anything like this, I know him."

"Oh yeah?" Malik sneered. "And how well do you know him?"

I frowned. "What's that supposed to mean? What are you saying Malik?"

He shook his head, then walked over to the floor to ceiling window. He stared out at the picture perfect view of the Capitol before he faced me again. "I'm done talking about Minister Xavier. This is church business and that makes it none of your business."

The volume of his voice had lowered, but his tone was even angrier and I feared that I had really pissed him off. Walking toward him, I watched him soften as his eyes soaked up my body that was barely hidden beneath the satin of my robe. I wrapped my arms around him and laid my head on his chest.

"I'm sorry," I purred. "I won't bring it up again. This is only about you and me really and I'm so glad you came by.»

With a sigh, he embraced me and we held each other that way for a few moments.

Then, I said, "I thought you were mad at me in church."

"Why?"

I lifted my head and looked up at him. "It felt like you were a little standoffish."

He shook his head as if I didn't get it. "This is the way it has to be, Pink."

I wanted to correct him. I wanted to remind him that I'd asked him to call me Sasha. But this funk that he was in—I didn't want to push it or press him. So, I just let it be.

He said, "There's no way that we can let anyone know about us."

Not a beat passed before I said, "For now, right?"

His comeback wasn't as fast as mine. He frowned a little, then, only nodded before he cupped my face with his hands and kissed me. A long, lingering kiss that felt like he loved me.

I was so thankful for this love, I was so thankful for this man. And, I made a vow to myself right then and there—I would never bring up Xavier's name again.

Chapter 16

Malik and I fell in to a nice routine.

I didn't get to see him as often as I wanted, but every Sunday, just a few hours after service, he would come to my condo and we would spend the rest of the afternoon and evening together.

It was always so romantic. Sometimes he would bring dinner, and sometimes I would make us something light to eat. But most of the time, we were in bed.

There was nothing like making love to Malik; I never knew what to expect. Sometimes, he was like that tiger ravishing me, and then other times, he was so gentle, so loving, he made me want to cry. I loved both ways, I loved all sides of Malik.

And, I knew that he loved me, too, because just two months after we began seeing each other, he asked me to stop by his office right after Bible study.

I had no idea what he wanted, though I suspected it had to be church business since he hardly ever spoke to me while we were in Grace Tabernacle. I followed him back into his office and half-expected Sister Stroman to be in there with him.

But once we stepped inside, Malik grabbed me, pressed me against the closed door and kissed me like he had never tasted me before. I wanted him right there.

When he finally pulled away, he said, "What are you doing tonight?"

I shook my head, since his kiss had left me breathless once again.

"Great," he said. "I'll be there in an hour."

"Okay," I squeaked.

As I turned to leave, he said, "And no need to get dressed. Meet me at the door, naked."

Less than an hour after he said those words, he had me pressed up against the window in my bedroom. It was the best sex of my life!

I was so happy when Malik didn't rush right home. In my bed, we snacked on popcorn and watched TV.

That was the first Tuesday that we were together, but it wasn't the last. Our routine now became Sunday and Tuesday, and though we mostly stayed inside my condo (which I understood) there were times when we would sneak off to Alexandria and stroll through the cobblestone streets or have a quick meal at one of the quaint restaurants.

It was a wonderful time, except for two things. First, the days were turning into weeks, and the weeks had become months. It was already September, and my hope was that Malik would start talking to me about when he was going to leave Sister Stroman. Not that I was being impatient; I knew that Malik had to take his time with this delicate situation. But, I wanted him to clue me in on his plans.

And the second thing that disturbed me was just about every time Malik and I made love, before he left the condo, we had to pray. Now of course, I didn't have anything against praying, but the prayers he would say—it almost sounded like Malik felt guilty and I didn't like that.

It was always the same. Malik would say, "Come on, Sasha, I'm getting ready to leave."

We would walk into the living room together, and he didn't have to say another word before we knelt in front of the settee. Holding hands, Malik would pray, "Lord, forgive us for this trespass, forgive us for this sin. And please deliver us from this temptation the next time."

It always made me frown. What was Malik trying to say?

But I never asked him. I was in practice to be the good wife. I was just letting him lead.

But though, I never asked him about the prayer, by October, I began to question him. It was one Sunday after church while he was still on top of me, that I said, "Malik, we've been together for awhile now."

He leaned down and kissed my nose.

I continued, "So, how much longer is it going to be before we're going to be together?"

He frowned. "What are you talking about?" he asked, rolling off of me. "You just said it—we're together now."

"I'm not talking about this," I said, covering myself with the sheet. "I'm talking about us really being together. I'm talking about husband and wife, together." When his eyes widened a little, I said, "That's what you want, right?"

"Yeah, yeah. Of course, of course. I just thought you understood that this would take some time."

"I do understand that, but can you give me any idea? I mean, you are going to have to do it eventually."

"You're right," he said, pulling me into his arms. "Let me plan this out. It may be another month or two, but I'll get this to work for us, okay?"

"Okay," I said, snuggling into his arms. Another month or two. Actually, that was perfect...perfect timing. Another month or two was Christmas. And I couldn't think of anything more romantic than getting my ring for Christmas!

Oh how wonderful this holiday was going to be!

Chapter 17

I woke up with a wicked grumbling in the pit of my stomach and right away I knew what it was. After Bible study last night, Malik had stopped by this little Korean BBQ place since he hadn't eaten all day. All he'd bought for me was a salad, but I'd taken a couple of bites of his beef and shrimp dish.

It had tasted kind of funny to me even then, but I just thought that was the way it was made. But now, as I felt the bile rising in me, I knew I was wrong. Even though I was moving as fast as I could, I barely reached the bathroom in time before the remnants last night's dinner spilled from me and into the toilet.

I stayed there, leaning over the toilet bowl, until I had enough strength to stand. But even after I rinsed out my mouth, washed my face, then ambled back into my bedroom, I didn't feel well enough to do anything except stay in my bed.

"I should've just eaten my salad," I whispered to myself as I wondered if Malik was feeling the same way.

I thought about texting him, but we kept our texts to a minimum since Malik was concerned about someone searching through his phone one day. The communication between us was truly limited to Sundays and Tuesdays, though I had a feeling it wasn't going to be that way anymore. Even though Malik continued to tell me that he was working on our situation, I just had a feeling that he was further along than he told me.

I really expected to have that ring on my finger for Christmas.

Rolling over, I glanced at the clock. It was just a little after six, but I already knew that I wouldn't be able to gather up enough strength today to go to work. I waited for just about another hour before I called Amber.

"What's up?" That was Amber's greeting.

"Girl, I'm so sick, I don't think I'm coming in today."

"Yeah, all right." Amber laughed.

"No, really. I really don't feel well."

"Well, you wanna know what I think?" Amber asked.

"No."

"I think," Amber continued anyway, "you're just holed up over there with Xavier." She laughed again.

Xavier. Although I didn't mention his name to Malik, I thought about him often. Especially since Amber was always asking what happened to him since he didn't drop by or call anymore.

She kept on, "Yeah, that's what I think. You've been hiding X over there and today, you two don't even want to get out of bed." Now, she laughed like she had cracked herself up. "Yeah, you better watch out before you find yourself pregnant." Now, she laughed like she was watching Kevin Hart on Comedy Central.

But, I wasn't laughing at all. *Pregnant?* Slowly, I sat up in the bed.

She said, "Well, girl, I'll cover for you at the office."

"Thanks," I said, my thoughts already elsewhere and then I hung up. For a couple of minutes, I just sat there, staring at the walls, replaying that one word—Pregnant.

Could I be?

It wasn't like Malik and I ever tried to be careful. He was the only man I would ever be with, and I knew that I was his only love. Well, of course, there was his wife, but I tried not to think about her too much. There was no way Malik made love to her the way he made love to me.

But right now, my thoughts weren't about Malik's wife. All I could think about was the possibility that I was carrying Malik's baby. Suddenly, I found the energy that I hadn't had before. I threw on my Victoria Secret jogging suit, my raincoat, and then made the four block trek to CVS.

Inside the store, I picked up every kind of pregnancy test I could find—the one that showed pink for pregnant and blue for negative, the one that had one straight line for negative, and then, the one with two straight lines for positive.

At home, I peed on every stick and then stared at the strips until one turned pink, the other had a dotted line, and the last one had two straight lines. No matter the test, the end result was the same.

I was pregnant.

For just a few seconds, I let that news sink in and then, I ran into my bedroom and grabbed the phone. I couldn't wait to tell my mother. But right before I pressed her number, I remembered. This was the best news I'd ever had to share, and I couldn't tell my mother. Nor my father. But maybe that was best. My parents weren't the first ones I should tell anyway.

Tossing my phone onto my bed, I wrapped myself in a hug. I was pregnant! With Malik's baby! My dream was coming true. This was the best thing that could ever happen to me.

Grabbing my phone once again, I pressed Malik's number. Yes, we never communicated this way, but this was something he needed to know now. The phone rang twice, and then went to his voicemail, as if he had pressed 'Decline' on his phone. I hung up without leaving a message. He was probably in a meeting, but that was fine. I could wait. In fact, if he didn't call me back, I'd even be patient and wait for Sunday.

I had four days to find the perfect outfit to be wearing when I told Malik that he was going to be a daddy. And in four days, our relationship would finally be official.

Calling the Four Seasons spa, I made my usual appointments, planning to spend the entire day there on Saturday. Then tomorrow after work, I would start looking for that outfit.

But today, I would just rest and revel in this news. I laid across my bed and let my thoughts wander.

Mrs. Malik Stroman. Reverend and Mrs. Stroman. Sasha Simone Stroman.

Come Sunday, the world would know that Pastor Malik Stroman was going to be a father!

Chapter 18

Glancing at my reflection in the mirror, I wanted to kiss myself.

I wasn't trying to be conceited or anything, but I knew that I looked simply adorable in my Versace Pink sheath. The dress was the rave of this season's Fashion Week. With its knee-length hem, and Peter Pan collar, it was certainly church-appropriate. But with the see-through back that dipped dangerously low, it was still a Sasha original. It was seemly and sexy at the same time. And then, my special-order Jimmy Choo four-inch, sling backs, and matching clutch, really set the entire outfit off.

Clearly, I had taken a lot of care getting dressed, but I had to. Today was the most important day of my life. Once I told Malik our news, my entire life would change. Knowing my man, I wouldn't be surprised if he wanted to present me right away as his love, the soon-to-be new First Lady. So I had to be prepared and I had to come correct. Show up and give Grace Tabernacle something they'd never had before—a truly fashionable, young, vibrant first lady.

With a deep breath, I grabbed my keys, wrapped myself in my fur-trimmed pink cashmere cape before I headed out of my apartment. All this week I'd tried to imagine what today would be like and I was far more calm than I'd expected. I'd been praying and praying for God to make the way clear, for Him to do what He'd done for the Hebrew children and to part the Red Sea and make what was about to happen easy for everyone concerned.

That's exactly what God had done. He removed my greatest obstacle—my parents.

I had been on my knees praying last night when my phone rang and the picture that popped up on the screen was my mother.

"Sweetheart," she'd said the moment I answered the phone.

Right away, I heard the desperation in her voice. "Mother, what's wrong?" I spoke and held my breath at the same time.

"I wanted to let you know that your father and I are driving down to Richmond tonight." Before I could ask her why, she explained, "One of my line sisters, you know her, Valerie Stinson, well, she had a heart attack and I have to get down there to be with her."

My mother had pledged her sorority twenty-five years before and yet, she was still close to her Sorors, especially her line sisters, the other women she'd pledged with.

"I'm so sorry to hear that, Mom," I said. "I'll be praying for Ms. Valerie."

"Thank you, sweetheart. We're going to spend the night in Richmond tonight and will probably come back late tomorrow or early Monday morning."

"Okay," I said. "Text me when you get down there. I love you."

"I love you, too, sweetheart."

When I hung up, I was really sorry about what my mother had told me, but as sorry as I was, I was equally relieved. That had to be a sign that God was answering my prayer. I was thankful because I hadn't figured out the way to handle this situation with my parents at church. Of course, I could have waited for Malik to just come to my condo the way he did every Sunday, but when had I ever taken the easy route? Plus, I really felt the need to tell Malik our good news while we were in church. I wanted to make this announcement to him while we were standing on Holy ground.

So with that call, my parents were the first obstacle out of the way and I'd be free to speak with Malik in his office once the services ended. Then, by the time my parents came home, Malik and I would be able to stand before them and together announce our plans for marriage.

Once I settled into my car, I pulled out of the underground garage, then turned my car in the direction of Grace Tabernacle. When I was just three blocks away from home, I did something that I'd never done before while on my way to church—I called Malik.

My heart pounded as his phone rang. I wondered if he answered, would I be able to hold back this news? I really wanted to tell him in person, but for some reason, right now, I wanted to hear his voice.

After two rings, my call went to voicemail. But that was fine. Once I heard the beep to leave a message, I said, "You know who this is. And I just want you to know that," I paused for a moment because I really wanted Malik to hear my next three words, "I love you." Then with a smile I hung up. That would set the stage for the rest of the day.

Parking was easy, of course; I just used my daddy's spot. And as the usher led me to the pew where my family usually sat, I didn't have the feelings that I usually had. Today, I didn't covet Sister Stroman's seat, since it would be mine next Sunday. Even when she glanced at me with a scowl, I was gracious and smiled at her.

I swayed and rocked with the choir, and marveled at how the sun glistened through the stained-glass windows. Everything was brighter and lighter. This was a golden day. Then, Malik strutted out onto the altar, and I felt as if my heaven had opened up. But then when he took his place at his seat, for the first time in weeks, my mind wandered to Xavier.

I wasn't sure what got me thinking about my friend. I wasn't sure if it was the empty seat next to Malik's or the fact that today was the most important day of my life. But in those seconds, I wished so much that Xavier was here. I wished so much that I could share my news with him. And, I wished so much that he would've been happy for me.

It didn't feel right to be moving on with my life in such a wonderful way without Xavier, but there was no use lamenting over this. Xavier and I were over. It was clear, that he was one of those friends who was only meant to be there for a season. And I had to accept that.

I took my thoughts and attention back to Malik and now that I was focused on my man, I took in everything about him. For the first time, I noticed that Malik wasn't wearing his usual robe. Today, he did something that he didn't do very often—he was wearing just his suit. His black suit with a blinding white shirt. But the best part was Malik's tie. His pink-striped tie. The pink-striped tie that I'd purchased for him on Thursday when I went out to Tyson's Corner to find my dress. In Neiman's I'd bought that tie for Malik and then had it FedExed to his office.

I knew he'd received my gift on Friday because I'd checked the tracking. But I hadn't expected him to wear it today! For me, this was just another sign. Truly, this was a day that The Lord had made—for me and Malik.

"Good morning, Church," Malik bellowed from the altar.

"Good morning, Pastor," the congregation said in unison.

"I'm feeling especially good this morning, praise be to God,» Malik said, and then, he turned in my direction. When he smiled, I thought I was going to melt.

"I'm going to ask you to bear with me this morning, because I have some special news...."

My body must've needed extra blood because I felt my heart pumping hard. I hadn't told Malik anything about our baby, but maybe God had. Maybe that's why he seemed so happy, like he was bursting with excitement.

"And I want to use the Word of God to share this news," Malik said. "Open your Bibles to Isaiah nine, the sixth verse, and read out loud with me."

Malik paused, giving us all a chance to find the scripture. I scrolled through the Bible on my cellphone and when I got to Isaiah six, nine, I was sure that I was about to faint.

There had been many moments on this journey when I'd had my doubts. Not so much because of my heart, but because of what everyone else was telling me. From everything Xavier had said, to my parents, to even Malik himself—there were times when the devil was using people to try to discourage me. But, I'd stood steadfast in knowing what God had told me, and thank God that I had. Thank God that I believed Him and I had faith when no one else did. Because God had clearly spoken to Malik through scripture, this scripture.

This was it. This was the final sign.

Malik began to read, "For unto us a child is born, unto us a son is given." He paused for a moment and I rested my hand over my stomach. "Church, I'm going to stop right here and ask my wife to join me here in the pulpit."

My eyes got wider. Was Malik kidding? Was he really going to do this that way? I didn't like Sister Stroman, not one bit. And I couldn't wait for her to be gone. But for Malik to bring her before the church this was—this was going to be embarrassing, humiliating. Maybe it was because I had so much joy, that I had compassion for Sister Stroman. I didn't want to see this happen to her.

Then, I thought about the role I was about to take. I was going to be Malik's wife. I had to learn to defer to him in all ways. So, even though for the first time ever I felt sorry for Sister Stroman, I sat up a little straighter, and nodded my approval.

Malik walked down the few steps and reached for Sister Stroman's hand to help her up to the pulpit. The two of them wore matching grins and I thought that was kind of weird. Maybe God had told Sister Stroman, too. Maybe she didn't have a problem with any of this. Maybe she didn't want to get in the way of God's plan.

The two of them stood side-by-side, holding hands. And then, time slowed down.

"Church, I've waited a long time, we've waited a long time. But, you won't have to wait.» Even from where I was sitting I could see how Pastor held Sister Stroman's hand just a little bit tighter, and they stepped just a little bit closer to each other. He continued, «We wanted to let our church family know today that Sister Stroman and your Pastor, me....»

The congregation laughed. Well everyone laughed except for me. My heart was beating so wildly, I could no longer smile.

Malik finished with, "We're expecting our first child." Then, he pulled his wife into his arms. And. They. Kissed.

All kinds of praises rose throughout the church: "Thank you, Jesus!" "Bless you, Sister Stroman." "Oh, my God, a baby!"

The praises went on and on. The pianist on the keyboard struck a few chords and then started playing *God Has a Smile on Me*.

Most of the congregation stood, and swayed, and sang.

But not me!

Just a few minutes before, my heart had been singing. Now I was sure, my heart had stopped beating altogether. While there were cheers all around me, tears streamed down my face. My tears were coming fast, but I wasn't worried about anyone noticing. There were others crying tears of joy—though mine were far from that.

Opening my clutch, I pulled out a Kleenex, patted my eyes, then stepped over the members who stood to the left of me. No one seemed to notice as I slipped out of the pew. The praise celebration continued.

I made my way to the lobby and really wanted to get to the car, but once I was out of the sanctuary, I could hardly move. But, I could certainly pray.

"How can this be, God?" I cried out. "Why would you let this happen to me?"

What was supposed to be the happiest day, had turned into a nightmare that I didn't understand. Malik couldn't be having a baby with her—not when he was having a baby...and about to get married...to me.

My world was falling apart and there was nothing that I could do about it.

I took deep breaths. I closed my eyes and continued to inhale and exhale. And a peace that I didn't understand came over me. With that peace, came clarity. There was no need for me to be upset. Malik had only done this because he didn't know about me. He didn't know that he was about to be the father of *my* child. Once he heard my news, there was no way he'd go through with having a baby with her.

That I knew for sure.

Turning back toward the sanctuary, I paused. Even though I realized the truth now, I still couldn't go back in there. Not with the way the members were still giving praise for this catastrophe. But I had to stay; I had to speak to Malik.

With surer steps, I moved through the hall toward his office and I felt better already. I had to remember who I was. I was Sasha Simone Jansen and things always, always worked out in my favor.

God always made sure of that.

Chapter 19

I felt like I had nothing but time as I sat and waited in Malik's office. I didn't think about the last time I'd been in here, just weeks before when Malik had pulled me in, pressed me against the door, and then kissed me with such force that I could hardly breathe. I didn't think about the first time we'd been together in here, when I'd taken him and made him melt with nothing more than my mouth.

All I could think about right now was what Malik had said this morning. His wife was pregnant. And he acted like he was thrilled about it.

I could have easily watched the rest of the services on the fifty-inch monitor that hung on the wall behind Malik's desk. Every couple of seconds, I would take in the image of Malik as he strutted up and down the aisles of the church like a plucked peacock. But, I couldn't keep my eyes on him for too long. I was too hurt, too furious to look at him. I just didn't know if I was angry at him or at God.

As I sat in his chair, the calm I'd felt earlier had faded away and my emotions teetered between anger, hurt, frustration.

But by the time the last song was sung in the sanctuary, I felt nothing but rage.

Now, I kept my eyes on the screen as I watched Malik open the doors of the church. Today, like every other Sunday, more than twenty people flooded the altar ready to give their lives to Christ, Grace Tabernacle, and Pastor Stroman.

Then, Malik gave the benediction, dismissed the church, and though the doors that led to the exit were in the back, women flooded the front, rushing up to Malik and Sister Stroman. They crowded around the two and before I knew it more tears fell from my eyes. Their celebration was supposed to be mine.

I lowered my head to wipe my tears, and when I glanced back up, Sister Stroman stood at the altar alone. That meant that Malik was on his way to his office, he was on his way to me.

Jumping up from the chair, I wondered what was I going to say? What was I going to do? But I couldn't get my thoughts together because I felt so shattered by his happiness.

That's what I was thinking when his office door opened. Before he even stepped over the threshold, I picked up the picture of him and Sister Stroman from his desk, and tossed the heavy frame across the room, praying that it hit him in the head.

I missed.

"What the hell?" Malik froze for a moment, took in the scene, then slammed the door behind him.

The photo may have missed my target, but I wasn't finished. I grabbed a handful of pencils and pens from the holder and threw them across the room, one by one, as if I was shooting bullets through a machine gun. "You bastard!" Those were my first words to the father of my child.

Malik ducked and dodged as he moved, until he stood in front of me. He grabbed me, then pulled me to his chest.

And that's when the floodgates opened up. I cried as if my life depended on it.

"Sister Pink," Malik spoke to me through clenched teeth, "get yourself together."

Sister Pink? Really? "How could you?" I cried.

"How could I what?" he asked as if he had no idea what I was talking about. Was he kidding me?

He added, "You shouldn't be in here."

I pushed myself away from his hold and backed up. "How can you do this to me?"

"Do what?" he asked. Then before I could answer him, he answered me. "Are you talking about my wife? Are you talking about the fact that she and I are going to have a baby?"

"Yes!" I shouted. "How could you do this? What about me?"

He looked at me as if I'd lost my mind. "Sister Pink, she's my wife," he repeated as if I didn't understand. And then, he broke it down further for me. "I love her. I have always loved her."

I took several steps back needing to get away from his words. "How...how...I thought you loved me."

Now, he stared at me as if he felt sorry for me. "Sister Pink," he said softly. He shook his head. "Before you, I had never cheated on my wife. Before you, I had been a faithful man of God."

"Well, something happened," I said. "Because you were far from faithful when you were in my bed, when you were making love to me."

He nodded, as if he agreed. "I fell into temptation. And I prayed to God to deliver me from that, to deliver me from you. And he has. He's blessed me, Sister Pink. He's blessed me with a baby."

I wiped my face with the back of my hands, knowing for sure that I looked a hot mess, and knowing for sure that I didn't care. "Well, then," I sobbed, „He blessed you twice."

I could see the wheels of understanding spinning in Malik's head. At first, his eyes narrowed as if he were trying to figure out if he'd heard me correctly. Next came the widening of his eyes, when he realized that he had.

This time, he was the one who stumbled backward, as if he were trying to get away from my words.

I didn't wait for him to ask me to repeat what I'd said. I figured he needed to hear it again. "Yeah, you heard me. I'm pregnant; we're going to have a baby, you and I."

Malik began shaking his head, slowly at first. Then, he whipped his head from side to side in total denial. The screen in his peripheral vision caught his attention and for a moment, Malik paused and stared at the monitor, where the camera was still set on the altar, where his wife stood, still holding court.

He didn't even face me when he said, "Sister Pink, we're not having a baby."

"I'm not lying, Malik," I shouted. "I'm pregnant. I can show you the tests to prove it."

Now, he looked at me. "Oh, I believe that you're having a baby. What I said was that *we're* not having a baby...you are."

My eyes narrowed. "What do you mean by that?"

"Exactly what I said," he stated in a tone that was as defiant as mine. "You're pregnant, and that has nothing to do with me."

It was a reflex of rage when I pulled back, and with as much force as I could muster, I slapped him so hard, my hand stung and began to throb. But my pain wasn't going to stop me from doing that again. This time when I reared back, though, Malik grabbed my hand in midair.

"Owwww," I yelled as he twisted my hand.

"Don't you ever put your hands on me again," he growled.

"Let go of me," I cried.

"I just want to make sure that you got my message." He gave me just a little more of twist, inflicting more pain, before he released me from his grasp.

"Now," he began as he straightened out his jacket. "As I was saying. That baby you're carrying is not mine." He spoke so calmly. "If you're looking for someone to be the father, maybe you should called Minister Xavier. You still have his number, right?"

I was trembling with hurt and with anger and at that moment, I truly could have choked the life out of him. But there was the part of me that loved him, still loved him. The part of me that had loved him since I was sixteen.

"Malik," I began, thinking that there had to be some way to reason with him. So, I calmed my voice, too. "You are my baby's father. I was a virgin when we got together, you know that. And, I haven't been with anyone since. You're the father and you need to take responsibility for our child."

If I thought my words were going to move Malik in any way, I was so wrong.

He stepped right to me and pointed his finger in my face. "I am not your baby's daddy," he said in a tone that sounded like he hated me. "And if you walk out of this office and tell that lie to anyone, and I mean, anyone, I will destroy you and your mother and your father the same way I destroyed Xavier."

I began to tremble once again, but this time it was with fear.

He must've seen my weakness when he said, "And if you don't believe that I will do it, you better think again. I will set it up so that your parents will lose everything. I've done it to people before, and I have no qualms with doing it to you." He stepped away from me, walked around to his desk, and looked down at some papers as if he hadn't just had this discussion with me. "Now, Sister Pink, if you would get out of my office, I would greatly appreciate it."

His words were polite, his tone was not.

In an instant, I relived every moment I'd ever experienced with Malik. From the moment he slipped that ring on my finger until now. This made no sense. But then, it made a lot of sense.

I didn't wait for Malik to ask me to leave again. I held my head down as I walked into the hallway, praying that I wouldn't see anyone.

But two steps into the hall, I bumped right into Sister Stroman.

"Sister Pink," she said in a sugary-sweet voice. "Were you looking for me?"

I shook my head.

"Oh, I thought you'd come back here to congratulate me and my husband."

There was a time, a few months back, when Sister Stroman and I had stood in this exact same place outside of Malik's office. Back then, I'd worn the veil of victory. Today, was totally different. Without saying a word to her, I walked away, this time with my head dipped low in defeat.

Chapter 20

I felt like I was comatose all the way home. The way my eyes stared straight ahead, hardly blinking, it was a wonder I could see through the tears that blinded me. I could have easily ended up in a crash, on the street dead. And right now, dead sounded pretty good to me.

The moment I entered my condo, I let the tears really flow. My prayer was that Malik would call me and beg for my forgiveness. But even though I sat in my bed, with the cell phone in my hand, it never rang.

And that made me cry even more. I cried so much, eventually, I had to go to sleep.

But I was up before the sun on Monday, still clutching my cell, still praying for that call. Still nothing. There was no way that I could go into work; I didn't even have the fortitude to call in. I didn't have the courage to answer when, at 9:30 my cell rang and *Power Play* showed up on the screen.

All I wanted to do was speak to Malik and though I thought about calling him, the only thing I had left was a little bit of pride. I was pregnant. He was wrong. He needed to come back to me. But, he didn't.

There was one call I had to take, though. When my mother's picture scrolled across my screen, I so badly wanted to let it go to my voicemail, but that move would have made my mother drive right over to my condo.

So, I answered, "Hi, Mother. Are you and Daddy back?"

"Yes, sweetheart. We wanted to stay longer, but your father had to get back for a meeting this afternoon. We'll be heading back there next weekend."

"How is Ms. Valerie?" I asked.

Then, I tuned out of the conversation as my mother went on about the damage the attack had done to her Soror's heart and that the prognosis was not good. And then, my mother shocked me with, "We did hear the wonderful news about Pastor and Sister Stroman. I have at least fifty texts from people from the church, isn't that exciting?"

I used the little bit of strength I had left to give an Academy Award winning performance. "Yes, it's great," I said.

My mother was fishing, I knew that. She was looking for any cracks in my armor, any sign that I still thought I was in love with Malik. So, she asked, "Why didn't you text me?"

"Mother, you weren't in Richmond for a vacation. I didn't want to bother you; I thought that news could wait."

My answer and my performance satisfied my mother. "That makes sense," she said. "Well, your father and I hope you'll come over for dinner this week."

"I'll try," I lied, "but this is a busy time."

"Oh, I guess so," my mother said. "Because of the holidays, right?"

I didn't tell my mother that the holiday issue of the magazine had been put to rest months ago. We worked four months in advance. But if she thought that Thanksgiving, which was just a week away, and Christmas would keep me busy at work, I would let her think that. It would be a convenient excuse that I'd be able to use for the next six, seven weeks.

When I hung up the phone from my mother, I went back to staring at the phone. Waiting for that call. I moved only to go to the bathroom, and even then, I took the phone with me.

But the call never came.

So what was I supposed to do? Here I was, pregnant, and not only didn't Malik want me, he was going to deny me and our baby. I would be a complete embarrassment to my parents.

The thought of that brought fresh tears to my eyes and I cried until I fell asleep. But when Tuesday rolled around, I knew there was no way I could stay in bed again. If I didn't show up to work, either Amber was going to show up over here, or my parents would start receiving calls.

So, I dragged myself out of bed, took a thirty-second shower, brushed my hair back into a ponytail and put on a black pants suit. My legs weren't steady as I moved about, finally grabbing my keys. As I stepped out of my apartment, I leaned against the door, wishing so much that I could just stay home. I didn't have the strength to walk, let alone think. I couldn't remember the last time I'd eaten, but the thought of food made me want to throw up. Somewhere deep inside, I found the energy to keep on and in less than a half an hour, I stumbled into *Power Play*'s offices.

My hope was that I wouldn't see Amber for a week or two, as if it was possible to keep her away for even two minutes. The moment I passed her cubicle, she was up and right behind me.

"Girl, where have you been?"

What I wanted to do was to tell her to leave me alone. But since that fight would take a lot more energy than I had, I just motioned for her to close the door.

"Are you all right?" she asked.

I placed my briefcase down and flopped into my chair behind my desk. I had never been one to share my life with anybody, but right now, I needed someone to talk to, someone who could listen to my pain. And the concern in Amber's eyes, the worry lines that were etched in her forehead, made me want to spill it all out to her. "I'm in trouble," I began.

Before I could say anything else to her, she rushed to my side, knelt down, and held me in her arms.

There was no way I had any more tears inside. So, I was shocked when I started to cry.

"What is it, Sasha?"

I shook my head.

"Is it Xavier? Did the two of you break up?"

Again, I shook my head and let the words pour out of me. "First, you have to promise me that you won't think bad of me. No matter what I tell you, please don't judge me."

She held both of my hands inside her own. "I would never do that," she said. "After all that you've done for me, I would never judge you in any way."

I nodded, inhaled, then exhaled my story, "I have been in a relationship, but not with Xavier. I've been involved with pastor."

She frowned for a moment. "Pastor Stroman?"

I nodded. Amber and her parents used to be members of Greater Tabernacle, but when her father's job had transferred him to Denver, Amber had wanted to stay in D.C. to finish high school. Her parents let her live with her grandmother, but when that happened, Amber only came to church occasionally and by the time we graduated from high school, she had stopped going altogether.

"So, you and Pastor..."

She stopped, so I could tell her more.

"We've been involved for months. I thought...." I paused wondering how crazy I would sound if I told Amber the whole story. But sounding crazy was the least of my problems right now. I'd acted crazy, and these were the consequences. So, I told Amber the whole story, from the purity ceremony to Malik's announcement on Sunday. I even told her about my relationship with Xavier, and how he had tried to save me from Malik and how I hadn't listened.

Amber just sat and listened. And like she promised, there was no judgment inside of her at all, though, she gasped a little when I told her that I was pregnant. "He's not going to accept my baby," I said, resting my hand on my stomach. "And so, I'm pregnant and alone," I sobbed.

"You're not alone," Amber said, hugging me once again. "I can't believe this happened. What kind of man is he?"

"I can't blame him," I said. "I've had a lot of time to think and I went after him."

"I blame him, Sasha. You're young. And not only is he the one who was married, not only is he older, but he's the pastor for God's sake! He could've stopped this if he wanted to."

I shook my head. "I just don't understand. I'm telling you, Amber, I heard God. I didn't make this up."

She looked at me as if she had a lot of doubts, though she wasn't going to say that aloud. That didn't bother me. I knew a lot of people didn't believe Christians when they said they heard God speaking. I was fine with that; you had to have a special relationship with God for Him to speak to your heart. But I'd always had that kind of relationship, and I knew what I heard.

I said, "God told me that the man of God had been chosen for me."

She gave me a well-how-did-that-work-out-for-you look, then said, "Well, what are you going to do? Are you going to tell your parents?"

I didn't even bother to answer that question, at least not with words. All I had to do was raise my eyebrows and Amber nodded.

"You're right. Your father will hit the roof."

"And if he gets into any kind of altercation with Malik, Malik destroy my father."

"Do you really think he can do that?"

"I don't know, but I can't take that chance. At the very least, he'll find a way to humiliate my parents with news of my baby and I can't let my parents suffer in any kind of way for my mistakes."

"I get that. So...." She paused and I was sure that I knew what she was going to ask next. It was the question that had been in the back of my mind since I'd walked out of Malik's office on Sunday.

She asked the question, "Have you thought about an abortion?"

I nodded. "I have. But, I can't do that," I said, unconsciously rubbing my belly. "It's more than believing that abortions are wrong; this baby...he or she is already a part of me. I was so happy to be pregnant when I found out last week, so happy that I was going to be a mom. So, how can I kill someone that I was so happy about just two days ago? How can I kill someone that I already love?"

"That's deep," she said.

"An abortion would be the easiest thing," I continued, "but this baby, my baby has nothing to do with the decisions and choices I made."

She nodded as if she understood, even though I knew she didn't. "So, what are you going to do?"

I shook my head. She kept asking that question, but I had no answer for her.

"Do you think you can call Xavier? Maybe he can help."

"Help me do what, Amber? Should I call him now, after he tried to warn me and I didn't listen? After I believed that he stole money from the church?"

"You don't believe he did that, do you?"

"No!" I exclaimed. "I never believed that. I was just going along with Malik because I was going to be his wife."

Saying that out loud sounded so stupid now. Why hadn't it sounded crazy before?

I sighed. "I don't know what I'm going to do, but calling Xavier is not one of my options."

"Okay," she said. "I get that. So, let's put together a plan. The first thing is, you're going home."

"I can't do that. I missed work yesterday and that was already the third time. I just got this job."

"And you're going to still have this job. You really are sick, Sasha. All any of these people have to do is take one look at you and they'll see that something's wrong. Your eyes are all swollen, your skin is blotchy, you look like you're going to fall over at any moment. You have to go home and get your strength up." She paused and then added, "For you and your baby."

Going home, and getting in bed, even for just one more day, sounded so good to me.

"And, I'm going to go home, too," she said.

"We can't both be out of work!"

"I'm not worried," she said, waving her hand. "I'm going to go home, pack a bag, then come over to you and cook you something to eat."

The thought of that made me want to puke.

"Don't worry," she said, as if she could see my face turning green. "Together, we'll figure out something that you can live with. I promise. So, this is what you need to do...call Bob, or go down to his office if you have the strength. Tell him that you're really sick and need a couple of days. Tell him that you'll work from home. You're the best junior editor they have, he'll be cool."

Then, Amber rushed out of my office to gather work for me to take home. I did what she told me, spoke to Bob, and he told me to take as much time as I needed—as long as I was working from home. We arranged for me to call in to the mid-week staff meeting tomorrow, and I told him that I would check in with him then, and let him know how I was coming along.

By the time I was back in my car, I had to admit, I was feeling a little better. Just talking to Amber had given me so much clarity, and I hoped that now, my thoughts would be clearer.

Amber was right. I needed to be stronger and I needed to be in my right mind. Because I had some serious decisions to make. Decisions that I knew were going to change the lives of everyone that I loved.

And, I dreaded it all.

Chapter 21

Amber did not disappoint. By noon, not only was she at my house, but she had settled in, made the bomb chicken soup, made me eat some crackers with it, and I didn't feel sick at all. At least, I wasn't sick to my stomach. But my heart, that was a different story. Now, I was eating and crying and eating and crying.

"I don't know what I'm going to do," I kept saying over and over again.

Every time I said that, Amber had an answer. "We're going to figure something out."

"But what?"

She just kept shaking her head.

After a couple of hours, she asked, "Are you sure you can't tell your parents."

"No!"

"And are you sure about..."

I didn't even let her finish. "I'm not having an abortion."

"So, if you're not going to tell your parents and you're not going to have an abortion, what are you going to do? Move away and have the baby?"

When she asked that, we both got quiet for a couple of seconds.

Then, she repeated it, but this time, it wasn't just a question off the top of her head. This time, she stated it, "Move away and have the baby!"

In theory, that sounded like a great idea, but it would never work. First of all, where would I move? And how would I move away from my parents? If I ever tried to leave in secret, they would come looking for me. Seriously, they would hunt me down until they found me and that's what I told Amber.

"That's true, but what about if we just disappear?" she asked.

"And how are we going to do that?"

"I don't know. I just came up with the idea," she said. "Give me a minute." She chuckled.

I shook my head. "I wouldn't want to do that to my parents. They would be so worried, and so sad." I paused. "No, I can't do that to them."

"Well, what about if you came up with a good lie."

I reared back a little. "I would never lie to my parents."

Amber crossed her arms, and looked over at me, like I'd just told the biggest lie ever.

"Okay, I do lie to them. But only when I have to."

"Well, this sounds like a good time to have to lie." She took a breath. "Listen, Sasha, the more I think about it, the more I like this. You could go away to have the baby and you won't be alone, 'cause I'll go with you."

"You would do that?"

"Yeah, why not? I mean, you're a trust fund baby, so I know we won't be living on the street."

For the first time in I don't know how long, I laughed.

"But seriously, it's not like I have this big important position or this big important life. I'll go with you and that might even make it sound more legit to your parents."

I thought for a moment. This could work. "But even if we do this, and I go away, I would never be able to keep my parents from visiting. I never came home when I went to Spelman, but do you know how often I saw my parents?"

"Well, they couldn't come to visit you if you went to Europe."

"You want to go to Europe?" I said already shaking my head.

"No!" she exclaimed. "I was thinking more like Atlanta, Houston or L.A.. But if we're going to lie, let's make it big. Let's make it so that they couldn't come every weekend."

I nodded, then shook my head, then nodded, and shook my head again.

"Look, no matter what, going away will give you a little bit more time to figure this out. It'll take away Malik's threat, and it'll take away this thing you have about not embarrassing your parents."

Then, Amber took the bowl that rested on the tray in front of me, away and she went into the kitchen to clean up. I knew she'd timed it to give me some time alone so that I could think. And the more I thought about it, the more that I thought it might work.

A part of me felt like I was being run out of town by Malik, and I thought about Xavier. This was exactly what Malik had done to him. Whatever had gone down between the two of them, Xavier had probably felt like he had no choice but to leave. Which was the way I was feeling right now.

But, I *wanted* to get away from here. From everything—my job, my condo, especially Greater Tabernacle. The only reason I wanted to stay—my parents. I could never imagine being away from them for an extended period of time like this. I would miss them terribly, but really, this was best for them, too. If I stayed, I risked embarrassing them with this pregnancy. And if I stayed, it wouldn't take long for my parents to find out that Malik was the father. That would lead to a war I didn't want my parents, especially my daddy, to have to fight.

No, for the greater good, it would be best for me to leave. By the time Amber came back to my room, and stood at the door with her hands on her hips, I was already nodding my head. I had the money, and Amber had the plan.

"Let's do this," I said.

She grinned, skipped to me and then bounced down on the bed. My stomach fluttered and I frowned.

"I'm sorry." She laughed. "I'm just so excited. I've never been out of D.C.," she said. "So where are we gonna go? Where does our adventure begin?"

I took a deep breath. It may have felt like an adventure to Amber, but it felt like the great escape to me. Either way you looked at it, the results were the same. I had to get out of D. C.. All because of Pastor Malik Stroman.

Chapter 22

It was hard to keep my secret as I packed and prepared for my new life. Amber wanted to leave right away, but there was no need for that. There wasn't any rush since I wasn't showing or anything. And, I wanted to spend the holidays with my parents.

"Okay," Amber had agreed. "We'll leave on New Year's."

"The day after New Year's," I said.

"New Year's Day," she said, as if this was some kind of negotiation.

I wondered why I had to compromise with her, but I did because to me, Amber and I were equals now. She didn't work for me, not really. We were doing this together and she was leaving her whole life to disappear with me.

It took us a couple of days to decide where we were going to settle. We talked about Houston and Los Angeles, but settled on what was safe – Atlanta, since it was a city that I knew. I wasn't too concerned about running into people I knew down there. It wasn't like I'd made any friends, except for Xavier. And, I wasn't going to be living anywhere near Buckhead in case my parents did decide to visit Atlanta on their own.

But while I would be living in Atlanta, my parents thought that I'd be doing a special assignment in Amsterdam. I'd thought about choosing someplace more glamorous like Paris or Milan. But my mother would have been on a plane with her black American Express the very next week. So, I set the lie in motion over Thanksgiving dinner.

I was the only child with my parents for Thanksgiving every year, my brothers spent that holiday with their in-laws. So over the six-course meal, I told my parents, "I may be going away."

"Really? For the magazine?"

I nodded, then took a sip of water to moisten my dry lips. "Yes. And this won't be just any trip. They asked me to go to Amsterdam...for a year." I sipped again as I took in my parents' shocked faces.

"Amsterdam?" they said together.

Then, my mother said, "Why Amsterdam? Why not someplace like Italy? Venice or Milan would be wonderful. I could move with you."

As she chuckled, I thanked God that I knew my parents so well. There was no chance of her offering to move with me to Amsterdam.

But her laugh didn't last long. She said, "Really, sweetheart, why Amsterdam? It's so far away and for so long."

I had an answer ready, but my father handled my mother for me. "Well, Sasha doesn't have a choice," my father said. "If the magazine wants to send her, then she has to go." My father nodded. "I think it's an excellent move for you."

"Yes," I said, so relieved that my father was doing some of the work for me. "When I come back, I'll be made a full-fledge editor."

Of course, it was a complete lie. I'd already told my boss that I would be leaving, though I asked if I could stay on to the end of the year to train someone. He had appreciated the heads up and had taken up my offer for training. I was working with HR now to find the perfect candidate to replace me.

"So, when will you be leaving?" my mother asked.

"The first of the year."

"Oh my." She pressed her hand across her chest and tears filled her eyes. "I'm going to miss my baby, my little Pink."

While my mother looked like she was going to cry, my father was just the opposite. He beamed as he said, "She's not our little girl anymore. We have to allow her to spread her wings so that she can be the best that she can be."

Once the lie was out there, it was full steam ahead. My parents told my brothers who all called me and promised that we would have the best Christmas ever so that I would leave with wonderful memories.

And the lie helped me to stay away from Grace Tabernacle. Every Sunday, I told my parents about some special meeting or some special call I had to take. And then during the week, I told my mother and father that I was going to Bible Study with Amber because her pastor was younger and I related to him more. Of course, Amber didn't have a pastor since she didn't go to church. But, my lies were piling up now, so what did another one matter?

Amber and I prepared for our new life. She found a three-bedroom apartment in the Midtown section of Atlanta, and when she started looking for a job, I told her not to rush.

"I'll pay you to be my assistant," I said. "At least until the baby is born and we figure this whole thing out."

My new life began to take shape and while there was a part of me that was embracing it, I hated to admit that most of my heart was still with Malik. I loved him and even though weeks had passed since my dream had been destroyed, if Malik had called me at any time and said that he wanted us to be together, I would've dropped all the lies and all the plans to be with him.

But that call never came. And time passed, taking me closer to the day when I would have to leave, when my entire life would change—all because I'd been duped by a pastor.

Chapter 23

I had pulled it off, at least for now. And I had pulled it off mostly because of Amber. All through the holidays, up until the day we left, I told Amber that she could change her mind if she wanted to.

"Are you sure?" I kept asking.

"Are you kidding?" she kept responding.

"But this is a lot to ask from you. I don't want you moving just so I won't be lonely. This was my poor choice and I don't want it to affect your life."

"Girl, please! This is an adventure. We're going!"

Amber had even come up with the greatest lie—what day we would tell my parents that we were leaving. There was no way my mother and father would just drop me off at the airport without going in with me to at least check my luggage. And once they did that, they'd find out that my final destination wasn't Amsterdam.

So, I told them I was leaving on the eleventh of January instead of the first. I was going to get on that plane on the first, then call them and tell them of the mix up.

Knowing that I was leaving the next day made it so hard for me to leave my parents on New Year's Eve. It was the last time I'd see them for months, and there was no doubt that the next time we connected in person, they would not be so happy with me. But I played it out, wished them a Happy New Year, kissed them goodbye and told them I would see them in a few days. Then, I drove away with my eyes filled with tears.

The next morning, Amber and I headed to the airport, both of us with only two packed bags. We didn't know how long we were going to stay, but I would make sure that we both had all that we needed.

I'd wanted to sell my condo, or at least rent it out, knowing that I would never return to that place no matter what. But with the lie that I'd told, my parents wanted to keep my condo in place.

"You'll be back in a year," my father said. "And it's paid off, so no worries. Your mother will go over there and make sure everything is okay once in a while."

So, on the first day of the new year, Amber and I arrived in Atlanta that evening. When I called my parents and told them of the early morning call I'd received from my boss, telling me that there had been a mix up with the tickets, and that I was leaving on the first, not the eleventh, and I only had two hours to get to the airport, my mother had cried.

"Oh, my God, so you left without seeing us? Without saying goodbye?"

"I didn't have any choice," I said, crying with my mother because I could hear her pain. "I had to go. They couldn't redo the ticket and it was too expensive to change it."

"I would've paid to have it changed," my father said.

"Well, it's too late," I told them both. "I'm already in Atlanta, about to get on my connecting flight."

It had been hard to hang up, but I promised that I would call in a couple of days. And I was going to call them. Just about every day. Right after I studied everything I could about Amsterdam on the Internet. I was going to work hard to make our conversations as authentic as possible.

Once that first call to my parents was over, I threw myself into my new life. Amber and I stayed in a hotel the first night— the Westin, not the Four Seasons, which is where I would've stayed under normal circumstances. But, I had to be a lot more responsible now, especially since I didn't plan to think about employment until after my baby was born.

Two days after we arrived, we settled into our three-bedroom hi-rise apartment and I was so happy that Amber had talked me into getting a furnished place. At first, I had thought that was a ridiculous idea.

"You want me to live with furniture that someone else has lived with?" I'd asked her. I couldn't even imagine that.

But Amber had ignored me, rented a fully furnished place in the luxury building, and all we had to supply was our own linen. As overwhelming as this whole trip was for me, I was so grateful that sheets, towels, and washcloths were all that I had to be concerned about.

It was the smartest move on Amber's part since I didn't really know how long I was going to be in Atlanta. We'd signed a one-year lease, but I hadn't figured it all out. I didn't know how long I was going to keep this news from my parents, didn't know if I'd tell them before or after my baby was born, didn't know if I'd ever go back to D.C.. But the great thing was that I had nothing but time to think about it.

While I didn't mind relaxing at home, after about a week, Amber decided that she had to get some kind of job. Not because we needed the money, but because, "I'll go crazy sitting around looking at you," she said.

So, while Amber went out searching for work, and going on interviews, my days were really simple. I spent most of my time wandering through Midtown, visiting the neighborhood Starbucks and strolling through the shops. When I was more adventurous, I ventured into the city.

My favorite destination by far, was Centennial Park. I'd spent many Sunday afternoons there with Xavier, hanging out, people watching. Before I'd met him, I'd hardly left the campus except for my beauty treatments. But during my Senior year, Xavier made me explore the city with him. I was thrilled when he'd taken me to Centennial Park for the Fountain of Rings show.

I'd been in Atlanta for only a month, yet, I'd visited the park three times. I wasn't quite sure why I kept going back there. Maybe it was because it reminded me of better days and a better time. When I was at the park, I didn't feel quite so alone. Of course, Amber was in Atlanta with me and she was great, beyond anything that I could have expected. But even with Amber there, I felt like there was something missing. Not a man—after Malik, I didn't know when I'd feel safe enough to be in a relationship. I did, though, feel like I was missing the safety and security...and love that I had with a friend like

Xavier. So, I guess that was it. Being in the park helped me feel close to him and close to the good times we'd shared.

Today, as I waited for the Fountain of Rings show to begin, I clicked on the Bible icon on my phone. The Bible opened up to the scripture that I'd been reading every day, over and over: *But you do not believe because you are not of My sheep. My sheep hear My voice, and I know them, and they follow Me; and I give eternal life to them, and they will never perish; and no one will snatch them out of My hand.*

I'd learned this scripture as a child, so I knew it by heart. But still I looked at the words, wondering if there was a message in there. My real question was how had I missed God? How could I have been so wrong?

The man of God has been chosen for you.

Even now, I would lay my hands on a stack of Bibles and tell anyone that God had spoken those words to me. So what happened?

I had to keep reading the Bible and praying so that I stayed close to God because the devil was telling me that I didn't know God's voice, that I had never heard him. That I needed to give up on God altogether. And a part of me believed the devil. Because clearly, I'd been so wrong about Malik.

I lowered my head, closed my eyes and whispered, "Lord, why didn't I hear you?"

You heard Me.

My eyes snapped open. It had been awhile since I'd heard God like that, so clear, so deep in my heart. Exactly the way I'd heard him all those years ago. But I'd been wrong then, could I be wrong now? And if that was His voice, what did He mean?

You heard Me.

Oh, my God! I was sure of it. I was hearing God's voice! So what was he telling me? Was I supposed to go back to D.C. and fight for Malik?

"Sasha."

The voice came from behind me, but I didn't want to turn around. Because the voice was so familiar. It was the voice that I wanted to hear. It wasn't until he called my name again that I dared to look.

And there he was. Xavier.

"Oh, my God." I pushed myself up from the bench where I'd been sitting. "What are you doing here?" I asked. Really, that wasn't the first thing that I wanted to do. I didn't want to stand there and talk. All I wanted to do was wrap my arms around him and have Xavier hold me.

As if he read my mind, that's what Xavier did. With a few steps, he closed the space between us then pulled me into a hug.

"What are you doing here?" I asked him again.

He motioned to the bench and we sat down together. When he held my hands and squeezed it, I had to blink fast to fight tears that were battling to be released.

"Don't do that, Sasha. If you cry, the tears are going to freeze on your face," he kidded. "It's kind of cold out here for February."

"I'm not gonna cry," I sniffed. "It's just that I'm so glad to see you."

"I bet I'm more happy to see you. I've looked all over; I'm glad I found you here."

"But how did you know I'd be here? How did you know I was in Atlanta?"

"I got one word for you—Amber."

Amber? What did she have to do with this? Had she known the whole time that Xavier was in Atlanta? And if she'd known, why hadn't she told me?

"Don't try to answer all of those questions in your head," he said, knowing me so well. "I spoke to Amber last night."

"She knew you were here? She didn't even tell me."

"I don't think she knew until yesterday," he said. "She told me that she had hunted me down. Hired an investigator to find me and she was pissed when she found out I was living in Atlanta because she could have saved herself some money and found me herself." He laughed, but I didn't.

I was in shock. I couldn't believe what my friend had done for me. But then again, I could. She had uprooted her whole life to come to Atlanta. At this point I didn't think there was anything that Amber wouldn't do for me and that made me want to cry. But I wouldn't.

"I'm going to have to pay her back. I hope she didn't spend a lot of money."

He shrugged. You'll have to ask her, but it couldn't have taken the guy too long to find me since I wasn't hiding from anyone."

"But, I didn't know where you were."

"Did you ever try to find me?"

I shook my head, then lowered my eyes. "The last time I saw you...." In the silence, he remembered that night, too.

"I wanted to reach out to you, but then, I remembered what happened the last time we were together."

He waited a moment. "What I remember about the last time I saw you was that I prayed for you."

His words and that memory made me want to cry again.

"Come on," Xavier said, as he stood and took my hand. "Let's go in there." He pointed toward the CNN Center.

Just minutes later, we were sitting in the Food Court, although neither one of us wanted anything to eat. All I wanted to do was stare at Xavier. I didn't even want to blink for fear that I'd wake up and find that this was just a dream.

"I'm so sorry I didn't listen to you," I told him.

He smiled. "I tried to tell you that I'm the wisest person you'll ever know."

I knew he was just trying to make this discussion lighter and I smiled with him. But, I was serious. "Everything you told me about Malik." I paused and shook my head. I couldn't even look at Xavier when I said, "Everything you said was true."

I waited for him to say something like I told you so, but he just kept his smile and stayed silent, leaving room for me to pour my heart out.

"I'm in trouble now, X," I said.

He rested his hand on top of mine. "Amber told me."

I waited a beat before I asked, "Everything?"

"You're pregnant," he stated.

I nodded. I guess that was everything. At least everything that was important.

"So, you're going to keep the baby?"

I knew my answer would probably change things forever with me and Xavier. He would never be able to look at me the same way and I was fine with that. As long as we could remain friends.

Again, I nodded. "I thought about it and once I realized that I loved my baby already..."

I stopped there and Xavier nodded, exactly the way Amber had when I told her the same thing. But I was sure that unlike Amber, X understood.

Needing to relieve the pressure of this subject, I asked, "So, why did you leave Greater Tabernacle? Why did you move back to Atlanta?"

He let a couple of seconds go by as if he was trying to decide exactly what he would say. "I got into it with Pastor. I confronted him about you. He denied it, of course. Denied ever being with you."

"Really?" I was more hurt than surprised. It had been more than six weeks since Malik had made his denials to me. But now that I knew who he really was, I was sure that he would deny even knowing me if that would benefit him.

Malik said, "I told him that I knew the truth about the two of you and that I was going to expose him. He fired me and said that if I ever said a word, he'd destroy me."

"That's exactly what he said to me!"

Malik nodded. "I'm not surprised."

"So, that's why you left." I wasn't asking him a question.

But he answered. "No. I wasn't afraid of Malik. He's a predator and a coward, he's not dumb. He talked a good game, but he didn't want to get in a fight with me."

I frowned. "So then, why?"

Not even a second passed before he said, "I left because of you."

My heart skipped a couple of beats.

He continued, "I had loved you for so long, but there was nothing I could do to convince you of that. You couldn't see it. And there was no way that I was going to stay and watch what Malik was going to do to you.» He shrugged. «I knew it would end exactly this way.»

His words made me feel so bad and so sad. I must have looked like such a fool to Xavier. And all the while, he loved me. Of course, I knew that he did. Not only had he told me, he showed me. And, if I had to admit it, I really did love him, too. But my eyes had been on Malik, and now, whatever had been possible with Xavier was now impossible because I was carrying another man's child.

"I'm so sorry, Xavier," I said, holding back my emotions. No matter what, I wasn't going to let another tear fall from my eyes. What would crying do anyway? I'd made this bed and ruined my life.

"Sorry about what?" he asked. "Sorry about what happened with Pastor, or sorry that I said that I loved you?"

"I'm sorry about all of it. I'm sorry I didn't listen to you and didn't see what was in front of me."

He nodded. "Sometimes, we have to be knocked upside the head in order for the scales to fall from our eyes."

"I believe that," I said. "Because trust me, I see everything so clearly now."

He leaned forward and covered my hands with his. "Really, Sasha? Are you seeing it all clearly?"

Now, I was the one who waited a couple of seconds before I spoke. "If you're asking me about Malik, I can see very clearly now. I can see him for who he is."

Xavier nodded, then, he frowned when I added, "But, I will never understand what happened with God."

"What do you mean?"

"I wasn't making this up, X. I know you and everyone else think this was just an infatuation, that I just got it in my head and went after Malik. But it wasn't like that at all. I know what God said to me."

Although I had told Xavier that I had heard from God, I had never told him the whole story. So now, I filled him in— from the purity ceremony to how I had prayed about me and Malik every day. "Even this morning, right before you came over to me, I asked God how had I messed it up, why hadn't I heard Him clearly. And God told me *again* that I *had* heard Him.

"So, yeah, I know being with Malik was an epic fail, but I don't get this other part about God. I'm telling you X, God clearly said to me that the man of God had been chosen for me."

Slowly, Xavier moved his hands away from mine and in that instant my heart broke. Clearly, my words weren't the one he wanted to hear, but I had to be truthful about this.

"So," he began, "the man of God had been chosen for you. That's what you think God said to you."

"That's what I know. I'm just confused because I don't know why Malik didn't hear it, too."

He peered at me. "Because he wasn't the chosen man. He couldn't have been."

"I know." I sighed.

"But don't give up on God."

"I'm not going to do that, but it's hard not to feel some kind of way when you think you've gotten a message and you didn't."

"Or maybe you did and you just got it mixed up."

I frowned. What was Xavier talking about? He was the one who was always saying there was no confusion in God.

Leaning toward me again, Xavier said, "God told me that the woman for me had been chosen."

My mouth opened wide. God had used the same words to him?

Xavier nodded before he kept on, "I had just graduated from Howard and was praying one day, asking God to bless my decision to go to law school, and to bless every part of my future.

"And during that prayer, God told me that even though I hadn't met her yet, I needed to start praying for the woman He had chosen to be my wife. He told me that she would come to me broken."

Don't cry, Sasha. Don't cry, I kept telling myself.

"But God told me that He would help me take those broken pieces and make her a stronger, better and wiser woman because of all that she'd been through."

When X stopped there, I frowned. I waited for him to tell me that I was that woman. I wanted so badly for him to tell me that. But he stayed quiet and my heart dipped all the way down to my toes. What did I expect? Even if Xavier once wanted me, why would he want me now? I was more than broken, I'd been a straight up fool.

But I wasn't going to be a fool anymore. I wasn't going to lose Xavier again. I would take his friendship and make that enough.

Then he stood up, and reached for me. He pulled me into another hug and in the middle of the Food Court, we stood there holding each other.

Finally, when we broke our embrace, he leaned back and said, "Come on. Let's go home, Sasha. Let's start putting together the broken pieces. Together."

And then, I did what I'd been fighting against all day.

I cried.

Acknowledgments

I thank God from whom all blessings flow. Brown Girls Publishing for allowing me the opportunity and platform to share my story. To my brothers Sonny, Larry and Joe and my three sisters-n-love, Valerie, Shirley and Sherese for cheering me on and taking care of me every step of the way. There are friends and then there are fighting friends (lol!) and these women wouldn't let me lose and I love them for it: Ophelia, Cynthia, Shirley, Alberta, Lacy, May and Shirley, I feel so loved that you ladies stuck by me.

My two sons, Nicholas and Chase for stepping up and pulling the weight for their mom when I couldn't do it for myself, from the bottom of my heart, I love you guys. Now, here's where it gets mushy so just bear with me...When my heart was broken into a million little pieces these people got down, picked them up, and placed the pieces right back in place, my baby girl, Jourdan Simone. Your strength and courage has gotten me through many days and nights. Knowing that you have been with me holding my hand, cooking me dinner, and making sure your mama was good to go, you're a warrior and a beautiful young woman and I can't wait to see the blessings that God has in store for you, thank you daughter. To Victoria, for being my mentor, my road dog, and a friend when I needed someone to listen. Thank you for your advice and guidance I truly believe that you're my soul sister.

And to Major Timothy Evans, my special man, because you're the truth and so real, and I love the way that you make feel, and if I'm a reflection of you, then I must be fly, because your light, it shines so bright. I love you (thanks India.Arie because these words fit perfect for my man)

I saved the best for last, I want my parents to know that they've been everything I had hoped my parents would be, my journey has been wonderful because of the love you continually give to me. Because in times of trouble, you hid me from danger, encouraged me to go further, you've been there for the good and bad, held me up and cheered me on. I love you mom and daddy....forever!

And just in case you're wondering, yes, my mother dressed me in pink and patent leather every day! lol!

If I missed anyone, please charge my mind and not my heart because every day of my life wouldn't have been the same if you weren't in it.

I hope you enjoy my first novel and I look forward to writing many more.

Made in the USA
Lexington, KY
04 April 2014